LEGEND OF AMOS

It was a quiet town till Cale and Jodie visited, not knowing they'd picked the wrong place. The legendary Amos was marshal there, had put himself out to grass a while with his old love Stella. Cale and Jodie landed in jail. But they were part of Whalebone's clan, his 'family', and the feuding and killing began. Whalebone wore a corset – but he wore a big gun also. And Amos had his notorious long-barrelled Colt Dragoon. Grotesque Ma Doombend got caught in the middle when one of her boys was killed, and her clan, too, were part of the final blood-bath – and even an old Indian called Lazy took part in that. . . .

BY THE SAME AUTHOR

The 'Amos' Novels
Black Heart Crowle
Bells in an Empty Town
Guns of Black Heart
The Hands of Amos Crowle
Amos Crowle, Widow-maker
Black Heart's Bunch
Hardneck and Amos
One More Sundown
The Greenhorn Days
Black Amos
Black Amos, Law-breaker
The Old-time Years
The Law of Amos C
Amos Lives!
A Shroud for Amos

Other Westerns
Savage Sunrise
Muldare
Men on a Dusty Street
Damnation Gap
The Plains Rats
Assassin's Run
Hannibal's Jump

Crime
The End of the Kill

LEGEND OF AMOS

VIC J. HANSON

A Black Horse Western

ROBERT HALE · LONDON

© Vic J. Hanson 1991
First published in Great Britain 1991

ISBN 0 7090 4299 X

Robert Hale Limited
Clerkenwell House
Clerkenwell Green
London EC1R 0HT

The right of Vic J. Hanson to be identified as
author of this work has been asserted by him
in accordance with the Copyright, Designs and
Patents Act 1988.

Photoset in North Wales by
Derek Doyle & Associates, Mold, Clwyd.
Printed and bound in Great Britain by WBC Print Ltd.,
and WBC Bookbinders Ltd, Bridgend, Glamorgan.

PART ONE

Homecoming

1

She had never seen him sleep so hard. Usually he slumbered like a cat, the slightest sound bringing him awake, wary, ready to act. She reached down and brushed away the lock of hair at his brow. Although his temples were grey the rest of his thick hair – and it was shaggy now – was raven-black.

She looked down at him and was overwhelmed by love, and a sort of sadness. Such a complex man. Fearless, ruthless, unpredictable, a lawman-gunfighter who had a short way with evil men. But sometimes a great humour in him, a warm philosophy. And a vein of kindness as pure as a streak of virgin gold.

His face was lean, finely lined, and of an aquiline handsomeness. She knew his body to be lean and hard, the muscular body of a still-young man with speed and co-ordination and power. His eyes were tightly closed now but she knew them to be of a curious bluey-grey, a sort of slate colour. They could be as cold as ice and pitiless, but they could also be as warm as sun.

He had not shaved and his cheeks were blueishly bristled, his moustache needing a trim, a few silver hairs gleaming in the thickness of it.

She remembered that when she had first known

him he had only just grown that facial adornment, which suited him so well she thought. Such a long time ago. He had been her husband's friend. Now the moustache had become part of him, part of the man they called Amos, just that ...

She heard the voice calling below. That would be Molly. She rose from her chair beside the bed and crept from the room, closing the door gently behind her. She went downstairs.

At the bottom Molly was bobbing up and down impatiently. She was eight years old and most of the time looked as if she were dancing. She was dark and slim like her mother and had big brown eyes. Her legs were long: when fully-grown she would be tallish. 'Mom,' she carolled, 'you said I could go to the store. But I haven't any money.'

'C'mon then, I'll give you some. And a list.' Her mother led the way into the kitchen.

After her daughter had gone the woman sat at the kitchen table and thought about Amos. He had told her not to let him sleep too long. He had been riding hard through the night and had needed a rest. He had been away almost a week and, having had no word, the woman had feared for him. But he had returned with two prisoners and now they were in the jail watched over by his deputy, young Rad Spink, who had been looking after the law in town while his boss was away.

A week ago the two men who were now prisoners had 'hurrawed' the town, and particularly the main saloon, and had shot a barman who was still struggling to survive.

The townsfolk would be glad that the hardcases were now incarcerated. Justice would be done. But such an uneasiness ... The woman in the kitchen felt it too. She rose and began to make coffee. She would take some up to Amos.

She was at the foot of the stairs with the coffee and some of the cookies she had baked the night before when he appeared on the landing above her. He was fully-dressed.

'I'll take this back,' she said. 'Come into the kitchen and have some breakfast.'

He grinned. 'It's a bit late for breakfast.'

'You've got to have breakfast.'

'Oh, all right. Rad won't expect me yet.'

He asked about Molly then and was told that the girl had gone to the store.

'It's quiet out there,' the woman said.

'Yeh,' he said. Then he asked, 'How's Latten, Stella, have you heard? I'll have to get down to see him.'

Latten was the barman who had been shot. The dark woman Stella said, 'He's still holding his own, that's what I heard. If he dies will both those men be up for murder?'

'I reckon so, but I'm no lawyer. My job's finished now, except for the reporting. They shot the saloon up though, both of 'em, and nobody seems to be sure whose bullet got Latten. They were crazy drunk.'

'Did you know them, Amos? Before, I mean.'

'No. Heard of 'em. Some sort of kin I heard, though they don't look much alike.'

'The town was so quiet before they came.'

'It happens, honey. Lots o' trigger-happy younkers like that roaming around, not particular about getting any work, raising hell just for the hell of it. And it seems like those two were well-britched. Maybe they pulled somep'n someplace else before they got here and I'll be hearing about that later. Pity I was down in the Mexican settlement when that shoot-up was on. Me on a peaceable mission too. And it was quiet like you said and young Rad was a-visiting his sweetheart.'

'Lila Keene,' said Stella. 'A sweet gel.'

'Yeh. By the time Rad got to the saloon those two were on the hoof. By the time he got his own horse they were way outa sight. As for me, I was almost way outa sight myself.'

'But you caught up with them and brought them back.'

'Yeh, I did that.'

He didn't amplify the statement and she knew better than to ask him anything more. His job was his job and he did it well, was notorious for doing *his* kind of job very well indeed. But he didn't talk about it.

She gave him ham and eggs, the eggs the way he liked 'em, browned and crisp on both sides. With small fries, and slices of sourdough bread and afterwards miniature pancakes with molasses. Between them they finished off the cookies she'd made yesterday, currant-filled and flavoured with orange and cinnamon.

They had drunk the coffee, but Stella made some more. Then she shared a smoke with Amos. They had one apiece of some store-bought packet of smokes he had bought as a change from his usual Bull Durham and papers, his makings.

Finally he puffed out his breath and said, 'By gar, Stella honey, that was a fine repast.'

He rose, grinning. He grinned pretty rarely but seemed to be doing it quite a lot this morning, a flash of white teeth almost wolfish beneath his moustache. His eyes were warm with his regard for her.

'I must go,' he said.

'I know,' she said.

He went first to the jail. Rad Spink was seated at the desk with his feet up. He was lanky and redheaded with freckles and a lopsided smile.

'Prisoners are still sleeping, boss-man,' he said. 'Hell, you wore the poor cusses right through to the bone.'

'I should've blown their asses off,' said Amos. 'I'm going to take a look-see at Latten.'

'All right.'

The wounded barman was in bed in his room back of the Street Place Saloon, aptly named as it was, being halfway down the main street of the town called Golden Bluffs, which had bluffs on its edge with something golden about them when the sun was right.

Latten had been living for years with a homely, faithful half-Comanche half-Dutch woman who sat beside him now and looked up at the visitor with eyes bright with tears. Amos was reminded of how Stella had watched over him this morning, though she hadn't known that he'd been aware of her presence. Why would a man fiddlefoot so much, he reflected now, when he had a good woman to care for him so? But that was a man! And he himself was surely the worst of all.

Latten was sleeping half-propped up on pillows, naked to the waist except for the winding sheet of white bandages over the heinous wound in his chest. The sound of his harsh breathing filled the room.

The woman said, 'The doctor says he can do no more for him yet.'

'He's a very strong man, *chiquita*,' said Amos. But he had to admit to himself that Latten didn't look too good at all. He guessed he would check with the local medico himself. That close-mouthed cuss wouldn't tell the woman much, though maybe that was all for the best ...

2

The two boys were hunkered down before a small fire in the draw when they heard the hoofbeats and they both drew their guns as they rose to their feet.

'Maybe it's Jupp,' said one.

'An' maybe it ain't,' said the other.

'Who else is it then?'

'How would I know, jackass?'

'It ain't Whalebone. He won't be back for days yet.'

'Yeh, an' I wonder what he's gonna have to say when he does. He's liable to shoot somebody.'

'It wasn't our idea to ...'

'Cut it! That jasper 'ull be on us any minute.'

They looked like brothers. Even twins. Both blond-haired and sort of cow-faced with pale eyes and plump redness. And stocky, bulgy bodies which matched the rest of them.

But the rider was small and lean, almost wizened, and considerably older than they. They greeted him with relief. He was the Jupp one of them had mentioned. But he didn't make himself as welcome as he might have done. He had bad news.

'I traced Cale and Jodie,' he said. 'They're in jail in a town called Golden Bluffs.'

'I told them not to go off on their own,' said one of the others.

'Hell, they took no notice of you,' said Jupp. 'Not after what Cale pulled off.'

'We all pulled it off!'

'It was Cale's idea.'

'An' Whalebone's gonna be hoppin' mad when he hears about it, like I said to Sandy here.'

'Yeh, he did! What did Cale an' Jodie do?'

'They shot the place up an' they shot somebody bad. A barman. Don't know whether he's daid or not. They picked the wrong town, I'll tell you. The marshal there is the character the border folk used to call Black Amos. But some of 'em liked him as well, strange though that seems. And he's marshal of Golden Bluffs, a real quiet town, a comfortable billet for Amos till Cale and Jodie happened along, them an' all their goddam money. Amos got 'em though ...'

'I heard of him,' put in one of the others. 'But he's old, ain't he, finished? If he got Cale an' Jodie they must've been as soused as hoot-owls at the time.'

'I dunno about that. But I don't sell Amos short. I was passing through Wolvers Creek when Amos cleaned that hell-hole out. I passed right through that town like a fart in search of a big bag. Amos and the Wolvers Creek clean-up. Hell, that's history!'*

---

* See *Black Heart Crowle*

'So he was a curly wolf. What's he doing ramrodding a quiet town then?'

'Having a sort of rest I guess. And I did hear he's got a woman there.' Jupp gave a snarling laugh. 'And now he's got Cale an' Jodie in his jail.'

'So we've got to get 'em out an' we've got to do that before Whalebone gets back. Or we're all in a peck o' trouble. So that town's quiet again, huh?'

'I guess so.'

'I wonder what happened to the money Cale an' Jodie got,' said the other bovine boy.

'You've still got yours, ain't you? But we've got to prove to Whalebone that we pulled off that job without his say-so because we figured it'd be a walk-over, too good to miss. So we've gotta get Cale an' Jodie outa jail, Amos or no goddam Amos. I reckon that old man's just gone back to sleep again or is having a good time with his woman now his town's quiet again. So we've got to get them two boys free before some townsfolk get fed up o' the quiet an' figure themselves a noisy necktie-party.'

'Leave me out of it,' said Jupp. 'I ain't about to put my neck on the block 'cos o' them two idjuts. I'm gonna try an' find Whalebone, try an' put things right with him.'

'Mebbe you ought to give him your cut,' sneered one bovine boy.

'He might demand some from all of us,' said Jupp. 'An' I guess mebbe he's entitled to it.'

'You mightn't find him,' said the second bovine boy. 'An' he ain't gonna thank you if you do. His private business is his private business.'

His partner said, 'And that job was our private business, ain't that right?'

'I hope Whalebone will figure that,' said Jupp

darkly.

'Oh, c'mon, he's just wiggling out.' And both the boys glared at Jupp.

They kicked out the fire, petulantly. They mounted their horses and rode off, leaving the older man staring after them. Then he said 'To hell with 'em' and rode in the other direction. He wasn't sure where he might find Whalebone, wasn't even sure whether he ought even to try. Whalebone would turn up in his own good time.

Jupp knew Whalebone better than most, knew his strange moods, his clannishness, his loyalties, his killing-furies. He was the *leader*, there was no gainsaying that, and he expected loyalty from all his cohorts. But he had his secrets ...

The rider came in, a temporary lawman Amos had known from way back. He had news of recent doings in another town. A bank had been stuck up just after a mine payroll had been delivered there. Some big mouth had obviously been flapping, or maybe information had been bought and paid for.

A bank teller had been killed and the gang had gotten away with a bundle. But they had been spotted, identified as they were taking off their bandanna masks on their way out of town.

'The man who identified them is an old owlhooter himself who don't get around much any more on account he's only got one leg. But he's got a long memory. You might remember him, Amos. Lafe Grindell.'

'Yeh, I remember Lafe. He had his leg blown apart, shotgun at close range, during a raid on a Fargo office. He was caught an' did time an' they took his laig off in the prison hospital.'

'That's Lafe all right.'

'So the raiders, how many and who?'

The visitor ticked them off on his fingers, Amos nodding at each name. 'Old Jupp, those two cowlike brothers or twins or cousins or whatever they are called Swede an' Sandy, an' another couple – I heard they were sort of kin too – called Cale an' Jodie. Five of 'em. And a sort of a clan. Maybe only old Jupp a sort of odd man out.'

'Jupp used to ride with that feller they call Whalebone,' said Amos.

'Still is, I heard. And the other four. And Lafe Grindell said he'd heard that. But Whalebone wasn't with 'em that day, so maybe there's been a break. Whalebone used to be a loner anyway, you know that, Amos.'

'Yeh, I know that, Rube. I met him a couple o' times, not in the line o' duty or anything like that though.' Amos chuckled, but not very humorously. 'Lemme show you somep'n, Rube. Come this way.'

The deputy called Rube peered through the bars of the cell and Cale and Jodie, who were awake now, blinked owlishly back at him. He backed.

'Hell, that's them all right. How in hell …?'

'They tried to hurraw my town. They shot a barman an', though I sincerely hope he don't, he's likely to die. They had plenty *dinero* on 'em too.'

'Their share o' the bank haul?'

'I guess so.'

'Goddam crazies. Shootin' up a town, and your town at that. Whalebone wouldn't have stood still for that. He's a pro. For him there's gotta be profit.'

'They were spending it. But I guess they got tired of that, or figured it too tame. And they were as drunk as two skunks.'

'Just the two of 'em?'

'Yeh.'

'So the gang must've taken shares an' then split up. I wonder where Jupp an' Swede an' Sandy are at now. Swede an' Sandy are allus together. I dunno about ol' Jupp. I guess you'll have to watch out for them young 'uns anyway, Amos.'

'I will, Rube. And I'm indebted to you.'

'You're purely welcome, Amos, you know that.'

'I've got to wait for my deputy, young Rad Spink, to come an' take over.'

'I remember Rad from when he was a sprig. I knew his paw ... I'll go to the saloon, get me some drink an' tucker, Amos.'

'I'll see you there in a little while.'

'Sure, Amos.' Rube took his leave.

3

Picking up Cale and Jodie had been easier than he'd thought it might be, though he'd been dealing with wild sprigs like that for all of his working life and had once been kind of a wild young buck himself.

He had trailed them to a little hole in the plains which had been dubbed Oatsville because a feller of that name had started a trading post there in the early days.

He had actually spelled his name Oates with an E and had been scalped and burned by pillaging Indians who took his wife and son away with them, leaving only the mutilated body of the man and the blackened shell of his establishment behind.

Nothing more had been heard of the wife and son. The Indians had been thought to be Apaches, so they might have taken the pair into the tribe and brought them up as their own. Funny varmints, Apaches. But it could've been Comanches of course. And if such had been the case they could've sold the pair over the border, the woman as a whore, the boy as a slave.

Later, a half-breed called Jika, an ex-owlhooter who had evaded the law and didn't have a dodger out on him anyplace, had settled with his clan, a mixed bunch of Anglos, Mexicans and tame Indians, in and around the shattered trading post and from this a little settlement had grown.

Jika was still around but much older than he used to be, and a hell of a lot wiser.

He and his people would trade with anybody, with and for anything. Food and drink, clothing, guns and ammunition, flesh (there were more women there now than there used to be), cattle and horses and pigs and poultry. But Jika in his twilight years hated trouble and did his best to avoid it, asking no questions, giving no answers or advice.

Amos had visited Oatsville before on various occasions. Jika and he had a wary respect for each other. The old man was as close-mouthed as an old maid with lockjaw and he just couldn't be pushed.

But on that particular morning he had been in a genial mood, had even seemed delighted to see his old *compadre*, the marshal of Golden Bluffs. As usual Jika had coffee on the stove and he poured a cup each for them. They sipped and they exchanged courteous small talk, Amos fretting but knowing that this was the only way the old man would operate, if he operated at all.

Anyway, maybe those two hardcases had skirted Oatsville. Or called only to pick up some tucker and water and had gone on. But, finally, Amos had to ask.

Jika curled his thick lips under his sweeping grey moustache and said, 'Those two!' Then he paused, eyeing his guest with those shrewd, black, shoe-button eyes which had nothing old about them at all, and asked, 'You want them, *amigo*?'

'I want them.'

'Why for you want them?'

Quickly, Amos told him.

Then Jika said, 'They came last night and after they had taken food and a lot of drink they visited the girl called Fat Sukie.' The old man chuckled, the mirth lighting his cat-face. 'She is enormous that one and she will take on any two men together. But those two were too much for her. Those two animals! She came to me only just before you arrived yourself, *amigo*. They had treated her badly. She has now gone back to her bed. And those two are in the bathhouse.'

He pointed out of the window against which their table was situated and indicated a long, low tent bathed in sunshine and said, 'I haven't seen them come out.'

Amos rose. 'I will try not to cause too much noise and trouble, my friend.'

'Just take them away,' said Jika.

He didn't offer help and Amos hadn't expected

him to do so, was gratified that the old man didn't figure he needed any, didn't blame him for following his usual policy of keeping his hands as clean as possible. His old roaring days were behind him, long gone.

'Tell the lady I sent you, Amos.'

The lady was fat. As he rode into Oatsville, Amos had seen a couple more. And of course Jika had mentioned the whore called Fat Sukie.

Amos hadn't been wearing his badge. Now he put it on and said, 'Jika sent me over. Where are the two men who came in together?'

She was middle-aged and not very handsome and her little eyes in their pouches of blubber looked scared.

'They're in number six,' she said.

'Both of them.'

'I think so.'

'Will you go outside, ma'am? Stay away from here till this thing is finished.'

'All right.' She moved with more than alacrity, her flesh shaking like a large sackful of rats.

The place was even bigger inside than it had looked from Jika's window. There seemed to be acres of grey canvas and the sun coming through and the heat, the smell of it, and the steam drifting down a long sort of corridor with the flap doors along one side, each of them numbered.

Amos padded down the corridor on strips of matting that seemed to be made of some kind of rush. He heard splashing noises, hoped nobody else was going to appear suddenly. Number six cubicle was at the end and the noises were coming from behind the flap door were the loudest of all, as if there could be a couple of bull buffaloes wallowing in there.

Amos wasn't a man who was oversold on stealth. He drew his gun and, with his other hand, reached out and swung the wooden-framed flap door aside.

He was surprised at the size of the bath, which filled the canvas-walled cubicle except for a sort of catwalk along the side. The bath was wooden and long and obviously well-caulked. There was plenty of room for two people in it and more, and maybe a couple of young buffaloes for good measure.

Cale and Jodie were one at each end and they were throwing water at each other like two kids and yelping.

Jodie was opposite the door and he saw the visitor first and became transfixed, mouth half-open, hands half-lifted, water streaming down his muscular body.

Impelled by his friend's gaze, Cale turned his head, saw Amos, the gun. The boys' own gunbelts were on a wooden ledge near Cale. With a defiant, reckless gesture, Cale reached out.

'Oh, no, boy, you don't want a blood-bath,' said Amos. 'Your pardner wouldn't like that.'

Cale was handsome and lean and well-built, with long hair that dripped oilily around his shoulders now. He had devil-may-care blue eyes and one crooked tooth which gave his features a boyish touch. A pretty evil boy none the less, Amos thought, as he said, 'Get out gently, boys. Nice an' easy now.'

Jodie moved first as, at the same time, Amos reached out with his free hand and scooped up the two gunbelts and slung them over his own shoulder. Jodie was paler-skinned than Cale and had little eyes and a broken nose and long arms like a gangling ape. He was awkward. But he made it without a trip or stumble, even managing to watch the lawman all the time, the levelled long-barrelled gun, Amos's notorious modified forty-four Dragoon Colt.

They knew him, these two. But still Cale was maddeningly slow, though Amos, with a sardonic smile, wouldn't be goaded, waited.

'What about our duds?' Jodie asked.

'Leave 'em!'

'We can't go out like this.'

'Why? It ain't cold.'

'It ain't fittin'.'

'Horse-shit! Move!' Amos backed out, gesturing with the gun. Cale came out first, didn't say anything. Both men dripped water. Jodie tried to grab a towel, dropped it at Amos's glare. The lean lawman looked as if he wouldn't mind shooting them both to save himself trouble. His sardonic patience had disappeared and he was all aggression now.

With impatient, violent gestures he shepherded them along the passage.

A fully-dressed man in black broadcloth came out of a neighbouring cubicle and paused, staring.

'Back off, buster,' snarled Amos.

The man saw the levelled gun, the gleaming badge. His eyes widened. He disappeared like a jack-rabbit in a hole.

There was no sign of the fat lady. But, as the marshal shepherded the two dripping, naked men across the sod outside the bathhouse, folks came out to stir and snigger, a few females along them, and Jika grinning like a fat cat from his window. And a fat girl who looked like she'd recently been worried by wild dogs. The boys' last-night sparring partner, Fat Sukie? Maybe.

But then Amos spotted the fat lady attendant and she was grinning. He beckoned her and she came over, skirting Cale and Jodie widely as they paused, glaring around them, covering themselves as best they could with spread fingers. Even Cale, a handsome buck in every way, didn't look so cocky now.

'Go pick up their duds, ma'am, if you wouldn't mind.'

'I wouldn't mind at all, marshal. Will I bring them out to you?'

'If you please.'

Soon she returned, tossed the clothing at the feet of the two boys.

Having spent all of his adult life around dangerous folk, Amos was far too intelligent to take fool chances. He stood away from the two, said, 'Put 'em on.'

They did as they were told.

While the populace of Oatsville jeered at them in various dialects.

Amos had never seen so many people gathered together in one spot in the settlement before. But Jika, not deigning to join the rabble, stayed in his window, grinning.

A man came forward with saddled horses, saying, 'I've got their nags, marshal.'

'I'm much obliged to you, friend.' Amos looked about him. 'All I need now is some rawhide.'

This was soon forthcoming. Jika didn't have to give out with his orders. All he had to do was stay in his window, grinning in approbation. The fat girl with the bruised face darted forward and spat in

Cale's face. He made a put for her and Amos gave him a glancing whack with the long barrel of the Dragoon, dazing him. He needed watching more than Jodie, so an early quietener might help. Amos grinned at the girl and told her to back off. She gave Jodie a nasty glance but made no move towards him, withdrew.

The two boys were tied to their horses so they wouldn't fall off, and that was the only concession the marshal allowed them. Ironically he saluted Jika, who grinned even wider, didn't bother to raise a hand.

'All right! Giddap!'

The folks parted, drifted away. The dust settled behind the three departing riders.

PART TWO

The Street

4

Jupp caught up with Whalebone in Santa Fe. He hadn't exactly been looking for him, had thought he just *might* be there.

Jupp had been uncertain. Now he figured he was glad, told himself that anyway. He wanted to put things right with Whalebone. He didn't want Whalebone to think that he, Whalebone's old friend, was running out on him.

He had the money, his cut of the proceeds of the bank job. He wondered whether Whalebone would want some of the money.

Whalebone was at Cornelia Dallahan's place, where Jupp had thought he just *might* be. And as Jupp usually called at Cornelia's place himself any time he was in Santa Fe, well ...

Jupp was welcomed in the ornate lobby, all red and gold, by Lola, the little Mexican girl he knew from way back, and it was she who told him that Mister Whalebone was there.

'He's with Miss Cornelia, I guess,' said Jupp.

The girl hesitated, then said, 'Did you want to see him special?'

'No-oo, don't disturb him.'

'Do you want to see one of the other girls?'

'No. I'll just stick around for a while.'

Lola did not offer herself. She never offered herself. Jupp had never seen her even arm-in-arm with a man. She was Cornelia's favourite. As far as Jupp knew, Lola could be a virgin, fresh as falling snow.

Cornelia would be looking after Whalebone in her own special way, in *his* special way. Cornelia was a big, strong, handsome lady who knew Whalebone best. He did not have anything to do with any other ladies nowadays. Cornelia knew him, bone and sinew and weakness and power and mood. Whalebone was in good hands all right.

'Can I get you a drink and something to eat, Mister Jupp,' Lola asked.

'Yes, please, honey.'

'We have some fine bourbon. And the big meals are just coming ready again, mainly roast duckling with vegetables and tomatoes. Then there are some of those spicy tacos that the cook does so well …'

'Yeh, I remember them.'

'… And cranberry and apple pie and coffee. And some new brandy Miss Cornelia has got in, if you want it.'

'I'll stick with the bourbon, honey. And the rest is fine. I didn't come in here *that* hungry. Not for anythin'. But, great saints, you've made me hungry now.'

'If you'll go in the dining-room please, Mister Jupp.'

'I'll wash up first if I could, honey.'

'Certainly, sir. You know the way.'

'I surely do.'

When Whalebone appeared Jupp had finished, was leaned back in his chair with a fine cheroot stuck out of his jib.

'So you're here,' said Whalebone, which was a favourite greeting of his that didn't mean anything much.

He was six foot or so and the way he carried himself so ramrod-upright, he seemed even taller, and lean with it, and hard-looking. A hatchet face and long hair of a sort of dark golden colour. Very smart in a black broadcloth suit and not a weapon on him in sight.

He walked very straight but didn't swing his arms much, though he could be fast with them if he needed to be, and with those long white prehensile fingers on the large but not ungainly hands. Whalebone had big feet, too, and he placed them one in front of the other, one-two, one-two, as if he were marching. You might have thought he had once been a military man. But he never had, though he often worked in a military way. He was a professional robber who had had his ups and downs.

A few years ago he had had a silly accident.

The gang had pulled off a raid on a bullion coach, even though it had been very well guarded. The job had been meticulously planned, as all Whalebone's jobs were. The boys had emerged from it unscathed and with a small fortune, leaving behind the upturned coach with some of its folk trapped inside and two dead men on the outside. The boys had been going well when the rawboned stallion ridden by Whalebone (and he hadn't been called Whalebone then) had stepped in a gopher hole or something and lurched and rolled, throwing the man heavily.

The horse had had to be shot. And the man couldn't walk, could barely move without crying out in terrible agony, his back shattered.

Jupp, a good man in an emergency, had taken

command. They had managed to get the leader onto Jupp's horse with him, and Jupp was certainly the sparest among them, and the badly-injured man had been held as best was possible by his old friend.

They had taken him to a doctor they knew who, having stepped way out of line once, wasn't legitimate any more, had to work under cover, a brilliant man gone wrong, a friend of outlaws and fallen women. But a well-paid one at that, a cynical craftsman.

The bandit leader had spent a month in the doctor's small hideaway hospital and the man had done wonders for him, had saved his life in fact. But it hadn't been possible to piece him together completely whole again and for the rest of his life he would have to wear a specially-made extra-long, extra-strong corset with whalebone and, here and there, steel also.

Then he was dubbed Whalebone. And he never seemed to mind this. He was notorious. He was powerful. He was the one and *only* Whalebone.

He could have retired of course. A rich man, he could have used his money in other ways. Jupp for one knew that Cornelia Dallahan had offered to take him in as a partner. For a handsome consideration of course. Cornelia was first and foremost a businesswoman.

But Whalebone hadn't wanted any of this or any other way of profitable semi-retirement and a life of respectability. The owlhoot way had been his way ever since he was a boy and it had been an exciting way and, all in all, a fairly profitable way, with long periods when a man could leave the trail and live high on the hog.

He enjoyed the danger, the movement, the planning, the daring, the triumphs, the occasional flops even, some of them funny. He had a sardonic sense of humour.

He liked the power, even the notoriety, bragging as he often had that no lawman had a dossier on him, a dodger for his arrest. He affirmed that nobody ever would.

And the boys, his assorted kin plus his old friend Jupp, were willing to go along with him on his sometimes merry, always dangerous, bloodsinging, bloodthirsty way.

That day Jupp told him about the bank job, Cale and Jodie's subsequent lollygagging, the shoot-up in Golden Bluffs, and the way those two idiots were now in Marshal Amos's jail.

Whalebone heard him out, then said, 'Sufferin' hellfire! They couldn't have picked a worse town.'

He seemed to be overlooking for the time being the boys' temerity in taking on a job, successful though it had been up to a point, without his leadership. First things first had always been his way. And Cale and Jodie were in dire straits!

And that wasn't the all of it. Swede and Sandy, those goddam 'cousins', were aiming to break the boys out of jail. Without any say-so from Whalebone either, or any help.

'That Amos, I don't know him well. But I know of him all right, by Jupiter. You follow me, Len?'

'Yeh, I follow you, Jake.'

They were using each other's first names now, like they used to.

'Those two idiots on their own are like infants, squawling infants, man. Compared to Amos that's all they are. Hell, if they weren't kin o' mine, both of 'em, *all of 'em* ...' Whalebone's words tailed off.

Then they burst out again. 'So we better go see about all this, *amigo*.'

Jupp reflected that that hadn't been his intention at all. Not at first. But he told himself that he couldn't let his old friend Whalebone down now. Besides, Whalebone wouldn't like it if he did, and when Whalebone didn't like anything his reactions were somewhat unpredictable, and sometimes lethal. Would Whalebone shoot his old friend, Jupp? Well, stranger things had happened.

'You had sustenance, Jake?' the small bandit asked.

'Yeh, I had some upstairs.' Whalebone's lantern-jib lit up with a sardonic smile.

'Just as you say then.'

'You all fixed, Len?'

'Yeh.'

'You an' me – let's go then.'

Cornelia was coming down the stairs, and Jupp called, 'Bye, Miss Cornelia.'

'See yuh, honey,' said Whalebone.

'See you, boys.' Comings and goings were part of the warp and woof of Cornelia's chosen life, and Whalebone was surely the comingest and goingest man she knew. They were good to each other though, good *for* each other.

Little Lola said '*Adios*' to the two men as they crossed the lobby. Jupp held the door open for Whalebone who marched through it, erect, soldierly, imperious, as if he were a state senator on his way to doings of great import. He was a bit awkward in getting off the sidewalk. Because of his disability he could not swing his body, had to turn all of himself all at the same time. But Jupp didn't try to help him. Opening doors was one thing, but putting a hand to Whalebone was another and would be bitterly resented.

Whalebone couldn't twist like he used to – they had known each other a long time and Jupp remembered those old days – but he sure as hell could pull fast and shoot straight. He was still the fastest man with a gun that Jupp had seen. But he had heard something of the same nature said about Amos.

Both their horses were at the livery stables and were soon saddled. Whalebone had always liked a big horse, preferably a stallion. Right now he had a rawboned, silver-grey feller with a nasty temper who wouldn't let anybody but his master get near to him and had even tried to bite Whalebone himself on a couple of occasions, earning himself a punch in the snout from the tall man, who had dubbed him Pizenhead.

Pizenhead's saddle was a heavy, ornate Mexican one with a high cantle which braced the rider's back and a taller horn for grabbing if he was in danger of falling off. It was built on a frame of thin wood and the leather was glowingly bronze and trimmed with silver with silver-chased stirrups, long ones to hold the rider's long legs, hug his feet, hold him, upright as he was, swaying slightly as they travelled.

The handsome horse, the tall handsome man in broadcloth: altogether an imposing sight. A senator? A general? A leader of men?

But Whalebone's companion, Len Jupp, had seen the tall man in his other guise, in his working accoutrements. Astride another smaller, and nondescript horse – but always a fast one – and wearing ragbag clothes and trying, if with difficulty, to make himself look smaller in the saddle. And with a scarf across his hatchet face or a mask across his pitiless eyes, Whalebone in another colour of his chameleon existence.

The tall man seemed to have been reading Jupp's mind and now said, 'I've got to get myself another horse for a while an' give ol' Pizenhead a rest.'

'Yeh,' said Jupp, non-committal as ever. Whalebone had the reins now like he always did.

5

Stella was on her own. Young Molly was down at the store again. She always liked an excuse to go there, and Stella didn't think there was any harm in that. Harriet and Benjy Kalen, who kept the store, were very fond of the dark eight-year-old. Harriet, to the sorrow of herself and her spouse, had never been able to bear children. They treated Molly like a daughter almost, or a niece anyway.

Two more tenants of Stella's place were out at their business. And Amos wasn't spending so much time there, hadn't done so since he brought the two hardcases back. With those two in the jail, the marshal was spending more time in his office, spelling Deputy Rad Spink. And also he had a new deputy, if maybe only a temporary one, a feller called Rube who had ridden into town with news and was pinch-hitting now as a sort of jailer.

Rumour had it that Rube had brought Amos the news that some friends of the two boys in the jail were aiming to pay a visit to bust them out. But rumour was rumour. Amos had taken the usual precautions, but he didn't seem to be worrying about anything.

He's a pretty unworrying sort of man, Stella reflected. He had deep thoughts, she knew that. He was complex – and sometimes maddeningly close-mouthed. She had learned to take him as he was, for she loved him very much.

She thought about the old days and of her late husband, Perce Rewberry. A gunfighter like Amos. First of all Amos's deputy and then a top lawman in his own right. Perce had been good. But he had been unlucky.* Then there had been Amos.

Time had passed and there had been no Amos. And Stella had settled in Golden Bluffs with her baby daughter, Molly. And Amos had returned, become marshal there.

A story time. A golden time now for Stella, in Golden Bluffs. But how would the story end? If only Amos was in a different line of work ...

She had never asked him whether ...

She never would ...

She looked at the clock and her face lightened. Amos would soon be in for his midday snack. And it was time Molly got back from the store. That little minx seemed never to have a conception of time.

* See *Black Heart Crowle* and *Guns of Black Heart*.

Yesterday she had come back with some good news though. The barman called Latten who had been shot by those two wild boys and whose life had hung in the balance was beginning to mend.

Amos stayed by the jailhouse of nights now, didn't come home at all. Stella wondered whether he was expecting something after all. Well, if something came it would most probably come by night, that was what anybody would be liable to think.

Stella heard the door open and shut. It was Molly, dancing in like a sprite. So soon.

'My, my,' said her mother.

'I saw Uncle Amos coming down the street,' Molly said.

'I'll get ready to dish up then.'

'Can I go back to the store right afterwards, Mom? Miz Kalen has been knitting a coat for me and she wants me to try it on.'

Stella knew that Harriet Kalen's knitting was famous. She sold examples in the store, among the other 'general' things, so many of them, so varied. No wonder Molly was so fascinated by the place.

'Miz Kalen spoils you. Her and Benjy.'

'They're nice.'

'Landsakes, I know that, honey. All right. But don't make a nuisance of yourself.'

'You know I won't, Mom.' Molly planted her feet firmly, looked indignant.

'I know.'

I'll have to make it up to them somehow, Stella thought.

'You're nice too, Mom,' Molly said, and Stella knew she was being teased.

Amos arrived, said, 'I haven't got too much time,

girls.' He often called the mother and daughter 'girls' when just the three of them were together. They were good together, the three of them, Stella thought. But Molly was the first to leave, excited about trying on 'the beautiful coat' that Harriet Kalen had made. And Stella and Amos shared a quiet smoke before the man left the dark woman alone again.

It was a hot day and a somnolent one. No cowboys around, all out on the range. The usual barflies in the saloon. In the back of the saloon, the Street Place, barman Latten's fat half-breed wife watched over him and smiled now with good hope. Marshal Amos had been right. He had called her *chiquita* and had said her man was a strong one.

The street was quiet. Were the town over the border, or near it where right now the hotter sun would be at its zenith, you might have decided that it was siesta-time. A cat lay in the sun, a dog in the shade. The kids were back in the schoolhouse after their midday break. The old saloon swamper, tired after his morning labours, sat against the wall in the shade, his head sunk upon his breast, his bald head gleaming, his wispy white moustache vibrating from his snores.

Another old man on his dusty burro came along the street and turned into an alley. This old man was called Apple and he was a half-mad but harmless ex-prospector who lived in a tiny shack at the end of the alley and subsisted on scraps thrown from the saloons and eating-places.

A single cowboy spurred his horse along the street in a cloud of dry dust and flogged the wind out of town. He had been due back at the ranch an hour ago after a morning off but had overslept in bed with his girl. The straw boss would wonder where the hell he had gotten to – and he didn't want to get canned.

His name was Green. He was using his real name now, and glad to.

He had once been on the owlhoot, just a kid then, little more than a horse-holder while his elders and betters did their business. He looked little more than a kid now, to his chagrin, and his girl sometimes called him her 'baby'.

When just outside, he saw the two riders coming towards him on the trail but not travelling as fast as he was, he slowed down also. Maybe two of the boys sent to seek him out. Oh, criminy!

But the two were nobody he knew ...

But then he did!

He had once worked for a couple of times with the notorious Whalebone. He used to brag about that, but he didn't do so now, kept it a secret instead. He had had enough of the owlhoot, the horse-holding.

He knew Cale and Jodie were in jail in Golden Bluffs.

And now – here were Swede and Sandy!

They didn't even look at him. But there was no mistaking them and the cocky way they went on. As if they were gonna blow up the world! Two blond, cow-faced, plump, stocky, red and mean-eyed sons of bitches. Green had always disliked them. More than Jodie and Cale even, though Cale was as mad as a hatter and it was probably him who had shot Latten back at the saloon.

There could be only one reason for Swede and Sandy visiting Golden Bluffs.

And now Golden Bluffs was his (Green's) town. He slowed his horse. Slowly he turned the beast around. The two boys were still staring straight ahead.

Green hesitated no longer. He set his mount at an even faster speed than that he had used for getting out of town. He went past the other two horsemen like a bat out of Hades, waving one hand as he did so, yelling 'Mawnin', gents', though it was already afternoon. He didn't know whether they answered him or not. His spine prickled. But nothing hit him.

They've always been kinda stupid, he thought. And riding into that town in broad daylight …

And did they know Amos was the marshal there?

Still, the town was so quiet. Maybe they had a point after all. Nobody on their guard as they might be at night.

Amos was coming out of the place where he stayed. At the sound of galloping hooves he turned. Green saw how swiftly his hand dropped to the butt of his gun and how his steel-grey eyes, alight in the sun, were fixed and steady, gazing at the cowboy as he dismounted with his story. Amos didn't ask questions though. And his tones were mild when he said, 'Thanks, friend. And you keep out of the way, will you, while I ask those boys what their business is?'

'Right you are, marshal.'

As luck would have it the Street Place Saloon was the nearest place of refuge. Green found his way in there.

'That cowboy was in a mighty hurry,' said Swede.

'Yeh,' said Sandy with sagacity, 'maybe he had an

urgent message for somebody.' He guffawed at his own lame joke.

Swede took it up and they brayed in unison. They spluttered. Then Sandy snorted, 'Cowboys! What brains they have are in their asses.'

They became silent then. Grim-faced. Oh, yes. Rescuers! Avengers! Hell in boots! The town was plain before them in the sunshine. It looked quiet. It certainly didn't make any noise. The hasty cowboy and his mount had disappeared long since and there was no echo of hoofbeats.

'What do we do first?'

'See the lay of the land first, huh? But not too long. I reckon we've come at a good time, *amigo*.'

They moved into the main street. They had seen many like it.

At first they saw nobody. Then the man stepped off the boardwalk and walked into the middle of the street and kept on, approached them.

He was tallish, lean, dark, with a slash of black moustache. He had a silver star on his breast.

He halted at last and he was right in their path and they reined in.

He looked up at them and he smiled thinly and asked, 'Can I be of any assistance to you two boys?'

For a moment they were nonplussed. Then Sandy yelled, 'Take him!' and dug heels in his horse's flanks so that the beast bounded forward. And then Swede on his mount wasn't far behind.

The marshal leapt to one side and dropped onto one knee. He was very fast. The dust from the horses' hooves swirled about him. It was Sandy's horse that narrowly missed him. Then Swede on his mount was abreast of the man in the street but a little further away.

Legend of Amos

The gun in the marshal's hand had appeared as part and parcel of his abrupt movement, his half-kneeling, crouching stance. But then his upper body became more level and the gun more level also, pointing at Swede like a gleaming finger. And exploding in black smoke, the hammer thumbed, releasing two shots, one upon the other.

The first slug brushed the mane of Swede's horse. But the man in his flight was literally propelled into the path of the other one, his own gun in his hand as he began to turn in the saddle. But the horse was carrying him. The slug bored into his temple and destroyed his brain, taking most of the top of his head with it at such a range. He left the saddle and went out of sight on the other side of the horse, his gun tracing a gleaming parabola in the air before hitting the ground.

Gun in his free hand, Sandy was using his reins with the other, turning his horse.

A little girl coming out of a nearby stores halted on the boardwalk, wide-eyed. Behind her a woman's voice screamed something. The little girl had something bright, a garment, slung over her arm. She opened her mouth and yelled. The words sounded like 'Uncle Amos!'.

Sandy swerved his horse in that direction, seeing out of the corner of his eye that the marshal had hesitated, his gun still pointed.

But he was obviously scared of hitting the child.

The horse's hooves made a thunderous sound on the hollow, splintered boardwalk. Leaning down from the saddle Sandy tried to scoop up the little girl.

She was fast, agile. She eluded him. But one of the back hooves of Sandy's horse caught her a thudding blow on the head and she crumpled. And Sandy, who had leaned too far over, was thrown.

He hit the sidewalk and rolled, his gun still gripped tightly in his hand. His horse galloped over him, missed him, went after Swede's horse and away from Sandy, both of them galloping away from the crumpled, bloodstained figure in the middle of the dusty street.

Sandy came partially upright against a wall. His legs were bent, making him a lesser target. The wall supported him, braced him. And the marshal, just off the sidewalk, was right in front of him.

Sandy heard the shots, saw the black smoke. He even smelled the acrid odour of cordite. He knew he had thumbed the hammer of his own gun and that its barrel was pointed at the man with the silver star, the gleam of which Sandy couldn't see anymore.

There were those two shots from that source, no space between them at all it seemed, and both of them driving into the full of Sandy's breast so that they hammered him back into the wall, the boards bending and creaking behind him, though he didn't hear them. It was as if he was being driven through them by huge mailed fists. And then the agony blossomed like a huge wash of blood, a gigantic flower, all one. He felt himself sliding. He slid into blackness. He was dead.

At that range the heavy bullets from the powerful Dragoon Colt forty-four had gone right through him. There were bloody snail-trails on the walls, red paint from the large doll huddled there, shapeless now and grotesque.

A tall, grey-haired man, storekeeper Benjy Kalen, was through his door, a shotgun clenched in his hands. But his wife Harriet passed him, running, then dropping beside the still small figure near their door, the colourful coat that Harriet had knitted lying there too.

Holstering his gun, Marshal Amos ran to join the two people as Benjy leaned his shotgun behind his door. At the batwings of the nearby saloon other folks began to appear, cowboy Green among them, saying to nobody in particular, 'They ought to have had more goddam sense.'

'The kid,' said somebody else, aghast.

'Yeh, the kid,' muttered Green. He joined the others in their anxious, questing approach on the boardwalk while the bloodied corpses, which might have been an attraction at other times, went unheeded.

6

It was night when Whalebone and Jupp bivouacked in a draw about two miles outside Golden Bluffs. They lit a small fire and made coffee and opened a can of beans which they ate cold with two spoons the little man always had in his warbag. As a general rule Whalebone didn't like 'piggin' it', as he called sleeping out. But tonight was an occasion which was a sort of means to an end.

Whalebone knew places all over the West where

he could rest up, or have himself a good time if that was what he was looking for. But now was different. They had talked, the two of them, and Whalebone had said that Jupp could go into Golden Bluffs in the morning to look at the lay of the land, as Jupp himself usually put it. Nobody took much notice of the little man, whereas Whalebone, whether known or not, would stick out like a tall preacher at a convention of midget Indians.

So at sun-up Jupp rode onwards while Whalebone waited and schooled himself to patience.

But the little man was back sooner than expected, saying that the town was as chattery as a wagon-load of monkeys. There had certainly been doings there!

Jupp became grave. 'Swede an' Sandy certainly beat us to it, old friend. But they ain't gonna tell us about that. They braced Amos an' he put 'em down. Folks ain't got around to buryin' 'em yet. They're still in the undertaking parlour. And Amos ain't there. He's taken Cale an' Jodie to Polesen where they're wanted more than he wants 'em. That's where we pulled the bank job, an' it was on Cale's say-so.'

'So you told me before. That Cale! He's crazy. I should've dumped him.' Whalebone hit the side of his head not too hard with the flat of his hand. 'Let me cogitate.'

Jupp left him to it but didn't have to wait long. The tall, lean man spoke his thoughts aloud. 'What do we do about Amos? He ain't in that town. And we can save Sandy and Swede from nothing but a hole in the ground. They're gonna get that anyway. So do we …?'

Jupp finished the last half-question for him. 'Yeh, do we go after Amos? But he's got a hell of a start, Jake. There's an all-night stage that calls in at Golden Bluffs at dawn an' Amos took Cale an' Jodie on that, in handcuffs. With a driver and a shotgun guard and, I'm told, a sort of deputy called Rube who it seems comes from Polesen or thereabouts and took the news of the bank job we pulled. Nobody else on the coach but them folks, so I heard.'

'All gunslingers, huh?'

''Pears like it.'

'That Amos! He's a canny one. But we can travel faster than a stage, which has to keep to the roads. If we cut across country, Len, we might catch up with it, even get ahead of it.'

Jupp looked doubtful. 'We might,' he said.

As they climbed out of the draw Whalebone asked, 'Anybody else except Swede and Sandy get hurt during that shoot-out?'

'If you mean Amos, nary a scratch. But I heard a little girl got stunned. One of the boys ran her down. She'll be all right it seems. Belongs to the woman Amos has there in Golden Bluffs. Sort of coincidence.'

'Yeh. I think you mentioned before that Amos has a woman there. That's interesting.' But Whalebone was doing no further cogitating, and they set their horses at a gallop.

Although it had been Whalebone's idea in the first place and Jupp had even been doubtful about the project, it was he who finally charted the route across country and over an area which he knew far better than his tall companion did, him being so much older, as Whalebone sarcastically commented. Whalebone had always wanted to be best at everything, pretended he was. It was one of his vanities. He was a very vain man. He had to get Amos. Both he and Jupp knew that now. But was this the right way?

Jupp, it seemed, had no further comment to make on this one way or the other. He led them across rough country and they did not actually see a road or a trail of any kind. Now and then they saw houses in the distance, ranches, smallholdings, small encampments, once a small wagon-train. They saw grazing cattle and a few horsemen. They were waved at in friendly Western greeting but didn't get near enough to anybody so they could speak to them, or even near enough to be recognized, they thought. Maybe it wouldn't do for them to be recognized.

Once, from a bluff, a snarling cougar menaced them, seemed about to leap. Whalebone drew his gun. He was very fast. But the snarling beast slunk away.

'Best,' said Len Jupp. 'A shot would carry a long way in these parts.'

'I know that,' said Whalebone caustically as he holstered his weapon.

But now they didn't talk much.

Until the smaller man said, 'I figure we'll come out on a bend where the stage has to go round slow. There are small hills there. But I dunno whether we can get there before the light fails. And, even if we do, the coach may've already gone by.'

They hadn't stopped for rest or tucker, just taken swigs at their canteens as they rode, and chewed on dried beef and munched dry-as-dust biscuits.

The sun was a red ball, lowering to the horizon.

The young cowboy called Green was back in Golden Bluffs again and paying another visit to the marshal's office. He was disappointed to discover that Amos was no longer there. Since the marshal's speedy putting down of Swede and Sandy, Green's regard for the man amounted to almost hero-worship.

Still and all, Deputy Rad Spink was there and Green knew him a whole lot better than he knew the marshal. Rad and Green had been tads together before Green went off on his rather dubious travels. But now Green was back in his home town and, like Rad with his Lila, had a girl there, the reason for his visits any time he could get away from his cowpunching duties. Sly visits sometimes, too, as Green's old friend Rad well knew. Green's girl Sadie was a bosom friend of Rad's Lila.

Green knew Len Jupp, knew he had been in town, and asking questions too. Jupp was gone now, hadn't spotted Green. But Green knew him as a rider for Whalebone just as Swede and Sandy had been. Three of 'em visitin', so close together! Was that more than coincidence?

Maybe Whalebone and some more of the boys were somewhere around not far away.

And Amos had gone to take the two prisoners, Cale and Jodie, to Polesen where they were wanted for bank robbery and murder.

'We ought to take a ride, Rad, me an' you,' said

Green. 'A sort of reconnoitre.'

'You ain't a deputy.'

'Well, that feller Rube ain't a real deputy, is he? And he's gone with Marshal Amos, or so you tell me.'

'Amos left me to watch the office, do the rounds.'

'You ain't got to watch the jail. There's nobody in there now.'

'There might be later,' said Rad.

'Horse-shit! This place doesn't need watching. The folks will watch it. It won't run away of its ownself. Neither will the town. Hell, if somep'n happened outside town, somep'n against the law, you'd have to go out then, wouldn't you?'

Rad allowed himself to be convinced. 'All right. Come on.'

They were about a couple of miles outside town when they hit dirt, though not exactly pay-dirt.

But just a friend of Green's off the ranch where he worked, or was supposed to be working.

'The boss's been asking about you,' the feller said. 'I suppose you've been lollygagging in town, sparking that gel.'

'None o' your business, Deal. And don't speak about my girl like that.'

The tow-headed boy called Deal, who knew Green's reputation as a hard young cuss, drew in his horns. 'No offence intended, pardner. You goin' back to the ranch now?' He looked at Rad Spink slantingly. Rad wore his deputy's badge.

Deal asked then, 'Is there some sort of trouble?'

Rad looked at Green and said, 'Mebbe he's spotted the man you mentioned.'

'Yeh.' Green described Jupp to Deal and the latter listened him out and then said, 'Yeh, I guess I saw that little feller. Early in the day, looked as if he was coming from town. I saw him join up with another feller. Tall feller on a big grey horse. And they rode off in the other direction, away from town I mean. The tall feller seemed as if he'd been waiting in the draw.'

'Let's take a look over there,' said Rad.

'I've got to go on,' said Deal, who hadn't been asked to accompany them anyway. 'I'm already behind-hand. I've got to pick up somep'n in town for the boss.' He didn't say what that something was.

'I suppose he asked you to look out for me too,' said Green.

'Well, yeh, he did mention it.'

'I'll be back at the ranch later on,' said Green shortly.

Deal went on. The other two went in the opposite direction and Green looked at Rad and said, 'I'm thinking o' giving up cow-pushin' anyway. Stupid way to make a living.'

'What else would you do then?'

'Oh, I dunno ...'

'An' you were talking of marrying Sadie and settling down. You ain't aiming to go off again, are you?' Rad remembered when Green had gone off before.

But much more recently Green had talked about a double wedding. Sadie and him, and his old friend Rad and his sweetheart Lila. Rad reminded Green of this now and Green said, 'Yeh. I'd still like to do that, pardner. But a cowboy don't earn much and he ain't at home all the time. Not that I'd like to be tied to any woman's apron-strings, y'understand. But ...'

'You're kinda mixed-up, huh, pizen?'

Green laughed. 'I guess mebbe I am at that. Mebbe I could be a lawman. I'm certainly as good as you with a gun.'

'Yeh, better even. But a lawman needs somep'n else besides a fast gun. He needs a level head.'

'I can be as level-headed as the next man. And I ain't afraid o' nothing.'

'I know.'

'Do you think Marshal Amos might need another deputy?'

'You'd have to ask him.'

They reached the draw and they dismounted and separated, ranging the rocky terrain. They found cigarette stubs, signs of horses, even traces of what might have been a fire, which had been scuffed over, half obliterated, hard to say how old it might have been, warm under the sun.

'It doesn't tell us nothing really,' said Rad disgustedly. 'And we know which way they went anyway, don't we, from Deal? I reckon that, working on what Jupp got from town, they've gone after Amos.'

'And the second one was Whalebone, I'd stake my pension on that.'

'You'll get no pension.'

'That seems likely all right. So what are you goin' to do now?'

'I've been thinking about that. Quickly, y'know. An' this doesn't change things. Amos told me to stay put so I'm staying put. Whatever comes, if those two ginks catch up with him, he can handle it. I'm goin' back to town.'

Green, would-be lawman, now-devotee of the legendary Amos, suddenly had a deflated air. He said, 'I was aiming to call in on Miz Rewberry to ask how little Molly is. But I guess I better get back to the ranch after all, us being much nearer to it now than to town. I guess I shouldn't run any more risk o' losing this job, till I get another one.'

'I was aiming to call in on Miz Rewberry today o' course,' said Rad. 'I'll tell her you enquired about young Molly.'

'Good.' Green had even thought there might be some sort of action in the wind. 'What I said, will you ask the marshal, Rad?'

'I will.'

'Fine.'

Green took his leave.

Rad went back to town. Things were quiet. He called in on Stella and Molly, who were glad to see him. Molly in particular was mighty excited about all the visitors she was seeing, some of them with presents. Rad, who was one of her favourites, gave her a tiny, pearl-handled pocket-knife which could be kept in her small, beaded reticule, or even fastened to a chain as a pendant: there was a small loop for that purpose. The knife had been given to Rad by Lila, to fasten on his watch-chain. But he had lost the watch, and the chain now lay in a dusty drawer in the office. Rad knew Lila wouldn't mind his giving the knife to the little girl, sitting up in bed now in a woollen bed-jacket that had been knitted for her by Harriet, childless wife of the storekeeper. Molly, like Lila, like Sadie, Green's girl, and many others of the female populace, spent a lot of time in that store, while the old men sat around the pot-bellied stove, smoking, minding their language.

7

They had ridden hard and fast. Jupp's nag was beginning to flag, and its rider said he himself felt like his bustle was worn down to the bone. Whalebone's rawboned stallion Pizenhead was still going strong, however, and its rider was still erect in his silver-chased Mex saddle, his hatchet face as skull-like as ever, implacable.

'We've got to slow down, Jake,' said Jupp. 'I've got to find the lay of the land. I figure we're getting pretty close to the place I'm looking for. See them small hills?'

'Yeh, I see 'em.'

'And the light ain't good now. I recollect I said it mightn't be by the time we get there. And we ain't there yet.'

'Quit belly-aching then. Lead the way.' Whalebone was making a small concession, like being only *half* boss-man now.

But he added a rider. 'It's still light enough to shoot.'

But you had to hand it to Jupp. He found the place all right. But, of course, they still didn't know whether the coach had gone by or not. They hunkered down in what they figured was the best cover in the rocks. And there was a billet for the horses behind them on lower ground and by this time even old Pizenhead seemed content to browse, behaving himself.

As Jupp had predicted, the light was far from ideal, particularly for fast and accurate shooting. But the coach, if it hadn't already passed, would be coming round the bend just ahead of where they lay concealed, rifles at ready. And Whalebone said seeing as how they'd come all this way, they'd wait a while, loaf a spell. They smoked, cupping their hands over their cigarettes.

Whalebone had said that even if they didn't get that pesky bastard Amos they might be able to create enough damage and diversion to enable Cale and Jodie to jump free.

There was still a flush in the sky from the sun they could no longer see. But there was a greyness, too, and a soughing wind had gotten up from someplace and the breath of the heat had cooled.

Jupp thought he heard a sound, said so, then said, nah it was nothing.

Whalebone said he hadn't heard anything.

But some sort of a sound there must have been and they were almost taken by surprise when the coach came round the bend.

Whalebone, naturally, had the quickest reflexes. He raised his Winchester to his shoulder and opened up.

'Get 'em off the road,' he yelled. 'Get 'em off the road.' And he shot one of the horses and the coach stopped, teetered crazily.

Jupp shot at the two men up top but didn't seem to have much luck. Sighting the rifle, he couldn't see worth a damn. And then the driver and the shotgun guard slipped down out of sight on the far side of the coach and fired from underneath. And folks opened up from the inside of the coach also.

Whalebone raised himself for a better shot but still had adequate cover. Jupp peered through a gap between two misshapen boulders, the barrel of his rifle resting on a small ledge. He figured he was pretty well covered. But he could not now see a lot of the coach, only the driver's seat, the guard's, both empty, and part of one window. And in that window, the canvas had been pushed aside and somebody was shooting from there at a rapid rate.

Jupp began to draw a bead on the window. Something punched him, hard, in the chest. It was as if a large chunk of the rocks against which he rested had become broken, had been propelled by some powerful outside source.

He was thrown backwards, his limbs in grotesque positions, his rifle leaving his fingers, clattering. Then the agony blossomed like a ball of fire and he knew he'd been hit and hit bad.

'Jake,' he called, and the name came out as a choking sound.

He was dimly aware that he now had his rear end facing the rocks against which he had been crouching. Forcing himself, he scrabbled forward in the direction of his horse, forgetting his partner now, forgetting everything but a need to save himself. Everything seemed to be getting darker ...

He reached his horse and hauled himself up against it. He retched, feeling as if his chest was coming apart. Arms went around him and he screamed. Out of the dimness he heard Whalebone say, strangely clearly, like a bell, 'I guess we better get out of here, old-timer.' Then he passed out.

*

Cale and Jodie were on the floor of the coach. They were handcuffed together and Rube, stocky and menacing, had a shotgun on them. Amos was at the window, his smoking gun in his hand. In the new stillness he said, 'I guess they lit out. I didn't actually spot anybody but I saw a rifle-barrel and I had me a pot-shot at that. Maybe I hit the cuss who was holding it.'

The driver and the guard were unhurt and so were the occupants of the inside of the coach. But they had a dead horse, still in the reins, while his companion stood dolefully regarding him. It was just a smallish two-horse rig but a stout one, pockmarked though it was.

The driver, who was called Jangles, was kind of upset about the dead horse. Actually, he hadn't been too pleased about the whole journey because, to avoid picking up any other passenger – this being a jail-trip as it were – he had had to make a detour. Thus he had had to miss out a way-station where he usually halted, sometimes to pick up a drummer or a farmer desirous of going to the town of Polesen which was Jangles' end of track on this particular stint, his usual one now, his *own*.

But recently Polesen had suffered a bank robbery and a man had been killed. Jangles knew all about that. And the two boys that Amos and his new deputy were escorting had been involved in the crime. Jangles couldn't really grumble about taking *them*. But he sure as hell could grumble about everything else, and he did. He hated to have his schedule, as he called it, mucked about.

Besides, what with the detour, and then this latest contretemps, they were now way behind time.

'Can we manage with one horse?' Amos wanted to know.

'I – I guess so.'

At this, the shotgun guard, wide-barrelled long-gun at the ready, joined his companion, looked about him at the silent rocks and asked, 'Who was that?'

'Who knows,' said Amos, non-committal as all hell.

'Maybe they thought we wuz carryin' bullion or somep'n,' the guard said.

Amos, unspeaking now, reflected that if such was the case those road agents hadn't done their homework very well. They could of course have been folks – he figured two at least – aiming to break Cale and Jodie loose. He had his suspicions, wished he had been able to take a look ...

'Get at it then,' he said brusquely, 'I'm gonna take a pasear into the rocks.'

Jangles said, 'Will you be ready when ...?'

'I'll be ready.'

He found scuff-marks which he figured had been made by riding-boots and, a bit further back, definite signs of grazing horses, two horses at least, he was pretty sure. And he found bloodspots, not yet dried, black splotches now in the fading light. He was gratified by this. But the riders had made good their escape and he knew it wasn't any use his going any further and it was time to return to the coach. Carefully, still looking, he retraced his steps. He saw nothing else.

The rest of the journey would be slower because of only one horse. The carcase of the other one had been dragged to the edge of the trail and quickly covered with loose rocks to try and keep it from the carrion birds and other scavenging creatures. Luckily, the rest of the trip would be a comparatively short one and across open land till their sight of Polesen. No chance then of another drygulch attack, unless the perpetrators were plumb crazy, and Amos didn't think they were, but just sort of reckless.

Anyway, one of them might be badly hit. Would they risk taking a shot-up man into Polesen?

8

Amos didn't know the marshal of Polesen all that well. He was a stolid, humourless man, more of a lawyer than an actual law-enforcer. But Polesen was a bigger town than Golden Bluffs and the man had a bigger staff, a bigger office, a bigger jail. In the latter there were already three prisoners but none of them of the vicious killer-outlaw stripe of Cale and Jodie.

Amos did his business, handing over the prisoners with courtesy and no flourish to the wary custodian. He had arranged to meet Rube, together with Jangles, and his shotgun mate, one Delly, at the biggest saloon, and to this he repaired, entering there as the evening was beginning to get well under way, noisy, convivial, welcoming.

There was little chance in here of asking discreet

questions about wounded road agents. He didn't think it would do much good anyway. He dived into the throng. He was no blue-nose. He had spent some mighty happy times in bar-rooms of many kinds over the length and breadth of the wide West.

He'd take a break.

It wasn't till later – though not much later – that he realized that this particular break was a break that he'd remember for a long time to come.

The West was full of characters. Of all stripes and colours and conditions. Colourful characters of varied hues and complexions.

The Doombends were characters, as who wouldn't be with a name like that? Some folk doubted whether it was their real name. Maybe one of the elders had picked it because he or she *wanted* to be thought of as a character. If such was the case, Ma Doombend was probably the culprit. She was the character to end all characters. But the rest weren't far behind.

The Doombends. Colourful characters. *Hideously* colourful characters!

You couldn't exactly call them a family, not now. More of a clan with Ma as the head, after Pa took seriously to drink and wasn't worth anything but spittin', as Ma herself was wont to put it. A clan consisting of sons and daughters and in-laws and nephews and all sorts of other human appendages, including the doxies that the boys brought in from time to time from the various towns and sink-holes they visited.

And sometimes Ma (who looked like a feller) took a shine to one or the other of these herself and

Legend of Amos

they stayed, semi-permanently anyway. Even the boys, one or the other, took a shine ... But in the main they had the sexual appetite and habits of stoats, and the doxies came and went like tumbleweeds in the wind.

The Doombend camp was in the middle of a circle of trees of various kinds. This had been a small wood until the clan took it over and cleared the middle out, using the timber to make grotesque cabins of various shapes which never looked permanent, gave the impression that the clan might at any time fold their tents, their inept efforts at dwellings and silently steal away.

But they had been there for years. Nobody could ever remember them having their billets anyplace else, the centre from which in parties large or small they ventured out from time to time to steal and pillage and kidnap and rape.

You could smell the Doombend encampment before you got to it and, riding in with the wind in his face, Whalebone got a real snootful. However, his companion Jupp, lolling in the saddle like a badly-filled sack of meal in peril of falling off at any time, was past noticing a mere stench.

Two of the boys came out with guns at the ready but holstered these and chorused, 'Howdy, Mr Whalebone', for Ma had brought them up to be polite.

Polite to their elders. And particularly polite to an elder like the notorious Whalebone. Even the boys, interbred near-cretins though they were, knew that if there was anything in creation that Ma was scared of that was Whalebone, whom she had once referred to as 'like some kind of evil speret'.

They were through the trees, with the two boys

leading on foot, when the bloodstained Jupp fell off his horse. At the same time, Ma came running out of the largest living-structure, which looked like a pile of logs and wattle with a leaning black smoke-stack and was surrounded by all kinds of putrid-smelling filth and detitrus.

Ma was a big woman and seemed to be getting bigger every time Whalebone saw her. She wore a battered wideawake hat with a ragged hole in the top through which a turkey-cock comb of grey hair protruded and wisped around her grimy, jowly, mean red face with the little eyes and the mouth with the pendulous lower lip revealing yellow broken teeth.

There was no denying it, Ma was a mess. She looked like a walking ragbag tied in the middle with rope.

Except for the boots.

They were higher than usual and reached up to the knees of her baggy pants (Ma always dressed like a man) and they were new and well-polished, the finest pair of leather high-boots that Whalebone had seen for a long time. He wondered what hapless traveller they had been stolen from. Many a traveller had wandered into this camp by accident and had never been seen again. Whalebone wondered how many bodies were buried beneath the sod among the trees.

Although Whalebone had never seen a Cossack except in pictures in magazines, he thought that Ma looked like a Cossack, around the legs anyway, and the boots were a mite too big even for her.

'Mister Whalebone,' she carolled, and she gave a little bob. If it hadn't been for the high boots she could maybe have curtseyed.

Legend of Amos 61

The tall, severely upright man on the big, dusty grey horse doffed his hat to the lady and greeted her as 'Ma', as everybody always did. Then with a jerk of his thumb he indicated the huddled figure on the ground and said, 'That's Len Jupp.'

'I thought it was.' She turned on her boys, raised her voice. 'Don't stand there gaping, you consarned jackasses. Get 'im inside!'

Like chastened puppies they hastened to do her bidding. They carried Jupp into the long hut. Whalebone followed but the smell of the place made him feel like gagging. He had been in some sink-holes in his days but this one was the living end. It had something that was all its own and that something was something the tall man didn't want much of. 'I'll water my horse,' he said and he led the beast over to the caulked wooden trough which was the only item in the area which seemed to have any real stability about it. Even the buildings, such as they were, seemed as if they were about to fall down at any moment.

The rawboned silver-grey stallion called Pizenhead made a token snap at his master and missed. 'Get down to it, you cantankerous son of a poison-mare' said the man.

He took a duster out of a saddlebag and began to wipe the beast down and, not heeding him now, the horse dipped his head and drank. 'Don't blow yourself up too much, you greedy varmint,' said Whalebone. But if there was anything in his black soul that he truly loved it was probably this hunk of goddam awkward horseflesh.

He heard a shout and he turned. And he exclaimed, 'Oh, Gawd 'elp us an' Betsy!' He couldn't remember Ma Doombend's Christian name, but her husband was called Nathaniel, and here he was, staggering, waving a bottle. An apparition out of a nightmare about goblins and elves. Small enough for Ma to swallow, though she hadn't managed to do that yet. Since he took to the rotgut in earnest ol' Nat had been too much even for her and as useless as a fart in the wind to stop a thunderstorm.

'Whalebone!' screeched Nat. 'Have a drink with me, ol' pardner.'

Whalebone opined that living with a strange crittur like Ma would be enough to drive any man to look into the depths of the wine and imbibe it. Ma might have been comely once but Whalebone couldn't remember when. He had heard tales though about 'callers' at the camp in the old days, rumours that not all the boys, and a few of the girls maybe, were not Nat's offspring; and, if truth were told, the brood did seem to favour their Ma more than they did their Pa.

Yeh, so maybe Whalebone did kind of sympathize with Nathaniel. But he sure as hell didn't want to drink with him, out of the same bottle at that. And the staggering apparition drooling like an over-fed infant and weeping too – flinging himself at the tall man as if to embrace him, missing him and falling head first into the horse-trough.

Pizenhead, this creature plunging in beside him and dousing him with water, was startled like crazy and acted in a characteristic manner. He jerked his long head around and bit Nathaniel in the ass. Probably the man yowled ... but the bubbles choked him. Had not Whalebone hauled him out of the trough he would have likely drowned. The tall man held him like a bedraggled rat and began to shake him dry. Pizenhead edged closer, teeth bared. His master hit him playfully, but still painfully, on the nose and said, 'Back off, you goddam cannibal' and he snorted indignantly and withdrew.

One of the boys came out, asked 'What happened to Pa?' didn't wait for an answer, went on, 'Mister Jupp's in a bad way. Ma's gonna try an' get the bullet outa him.'

The slug had been in one side of Len's chest, Whalebone knew that. 'Hell!' he snorted and he dropped the dripping Nat in a heap and followed the boy back to the long cabin.

They were near the door when they heard Len Jupp scream, a hideous banshee sound that faded to a bubbling gurgle. Then died altogether. But Ma came out of the cabin with a clatter, a large bloodstained kitchen knife in her fist.

'He was too far gone, Mister Whalebone,' she said. 'I couldn't save him.'

Whalebone didn't say anything. He moved a little closer, very upright, soldierly, but with a light tread. He hit her with a looping right hand, a powerful blow full in her blubbery lips. Her feet went from under her, long boots and all, and she hit the ground like a sack full of grits and thick molasses. Whalebone drew his gun. The boy stood gaping.

Two more boys came out of the cabin and halted. They stood gaping too, and behind them a girl suddenly appeared, the first one Whalebone had seen in the camp today. She looked as open-mouthed and cretinous as the boys did.

The tall man, still as erect as a pole, pointed the

gun at the big woman on the ground, the dust settling around her.

'Bury Len Jupp an' bury him deep,' he said. 'He hasn't been here, y'understand? You ain't seen him. And you ain't seen me either. Understand? *Understand?*'

Ma didn't say anything. She just lay there with her head lifted a little now, blood running from her bursted mouth and down her chin. And now she started to nod her head and she kept nodding it, but she didn't look upwards at the tall man. Nobody else near moved even a fraction but other folk were appearing from other places. Like curs an' bitches, thought Whalebone. Like curs an' bitches!

He holstered his gun and turned about and marched over to his horse, who seemed to look at him with that curious, mocking way that he had but stood docilely and allowed him to mount.

'C'mon, you' said Whalebone and jerked the reins. Pizenhead began to move.

Behind them a screechy voice yelled, 'Jake. *Jake!* Whalebone, you fancy, corseted son-of-a-bitch, *you!*'

It was old Nathaniel, curiously articulate suddenly, as a drunk can be, waving-fist fighting-fit; but if he'd had a gun he would've probably shot somebody else instead of his 'ol' pard' Jake, called Whalebone.

The tall man, erect in the saddle, did not look back. He set the horse at a gallop.

He went to Sante Fe. He returned to Cornelia Dallahan's place. He told Cornelia about Len Jupp's death and she cried a bit, and she gentled him, and then she pleasured him as only she could.

The boys were gone. Len was gone. Whalebone knew he could pick up other boys, but he decided he didn't want to do that yet. He had plenty *dinero*, and there was always more here with Cornelia. He decided to stay with her, just for a little while.

And then there would be scores to settle. One score in particular that would *have* to be settled. To make an end of it one way or the other ...

9

Jangles the coach-driver and Delly the shotgun guard were men of about the same age and build as Amos, give or take a year or so, a pound or so. Amos's surrogate deputy, Rube, was a mite younger, shorter, stocky, built like a brick privy, and there were a few of these in Polesen, courtesy of the city fathers. The one behind the saloon, however, was a leaning, ramshackle edifice which had seen a lot of wear and tear, was pockmarked with bullet-holes and spattered with debris. It hadn't seen a lot of traffic so far this night, that would come later.

But already the saloon was getting full to overflowing and the booze ran like mountain streams swollen by the rain. Over in the corner the dealers were doing well and the roulette-wheel spun and clicked. Every now and then the tinkle of a piano cut in through the general cacophony and somebody tried to sing raucously, hideously out of tune. The piano-player, in obligatory striped vest and with a black derby hat tilted on the side of his head, had a little dais all to himself on which he perched with his long instrument.

A drunk leaned against the piano and attempted to warble a song that was nothing like the one that the piano-player was rendering, until the latter, who looked capable of pounding people as hard as he pounded the keys, gave the noisy intruder a push. Amid laughter the drunk was lost in the crowd among britches and boots, was hauled to his feet and pointed at the bar once more.

On his bumbling way to his objective he was waylaid by a percentage girl and steered to a table where, to her chagrin, he fell asleep with his head in a pool of liquor. Already the place was redolent of spilled hooch – among other things. A hot room full of cowboys and horsemen, some of whom hadn't washed since they came off the range, didn't actually smell like ashes of roses, so the mixed odours of booze and smoke and the perfume of the mingling doxies was a sort of bonus, or an antidote.

Amos wended his way through the throng, courteously, not too pushy. Some folks greeted him. Others edged surreptitiously and silently out of his way. A girl accosted him and he said gently 'Not right now, honey' and continued on his way. And finally he reached his three friends at the bar and was poured a drink from an already half-killed bottle of rye.

'Everything all right, Amos?' Rube asked.

'Yup.'

Their number made up now, they found an

empty table and settled down to some steady drinking.

Now they were for the most part below the flux of the restless, away from any long ears that might have been ranked along the bar, the ensuing conversation was inevitable. Delly, the somewhat cantankerous shotgun guard, immediately brought up the subject which had bedevilled him on the trail, saying that as the prisoners Cale and Jodie were well-known Whalebone boys it was probably Whalebone, or folks working on his behalf, who had pulled off the ambush.

Amos wasn't so non-committal now as he had been on the trail. He said, 'It's a likely thing I guess. But as we didn't see anybody or find any clues that might point to anybody we've got nothing to go on.'

Jangles the driver said, 'Maybe there's some way of finding out. If somebody knew where Whalebone was …' He tailed off, the other men watching him.

Amos said flatly, 'As far as I know nobody's got anything on Whalebone yet. He's a cunnin', corseted ol' bastard. I don't think there's a dodger on him anyplace. If there is I ain't seen it. Stupid he ain't. If he was involved in that hold-up he'll be miles away by now. Come to think of it, that ambush, the way it was fixed, that was pretty stupid. I dunno …'

He tailed off. They looked at him.

Then Rube said, 'Oh, hell, let's drop it for now. What's the use of arguin' about it?'

'Who's arguin'?' said Jangles.

'Besides,' said Rube. 'We're out of booze. This bottle's plumb empty.' A passing girl in flounces caught his eye and he called her over. She swayed to him, smiling her brittle smile. 'Get us another bottle of this rotgut, will you?' he said.

She said, 'It's not my function to carry drinks.'

'Function!' said Rube. 'That's a fine, fancy word. Ain't that a fine, fancy word, fellers?'

'It is', 'Yeh', they chorused.

'What *is* your function, honey?' asked Rube. Then he added hastily, 'Don't answer that. Just bend this way a leetle, huh.'

She bent. He reached. In his fingers were a clutch of greenbacks. 'You'll find there's more than a mite extra there, my pretty, an' it's all yours for a bottle. Just a bottle. Me an' my friends just want a few quiet imbibes an' that's all.'

'Imbibes,' mocked Jangles. 'That's a fine, fancy word, ain't it, fellers?'

'Yeh,' chorused the other two.

'I ain't ever heard that word before,' said Amos.

At this time Rube was busily stuffing the banknotes down the girl's décolletage, while she giggled, quite tractable now, her breasts nudging his hand like two plump and playful puppies.

'Goddamit, c'mon,' snorted Delly. 'I'm thirsty.'

Grinning, Rube made it, and the girl swayed away, while he called after her, 'Don't get lost, y'hear!'

'Hell, I thought you wuz tryin' to get to her navel,' Jangles said.

She came back with the bottles. And now the brassy-haired filly was all smiles for Rube. Evidently the change left over had been handsome. As she turned away he patted her bustled rear and she inclined her head and gave him a roguish sidelong glance.

That was why Rube disappeared not so long

afterwards, and Jangles commented, 'Randy little cuss'.

Amos chuckled, said, 'He's earned it I guess.'

The populace swirled around the small table like waves of the sea but the three men, with their booze and their smokes and their now-desultory chatter – mainly colourful anecdotes of things passed – paid it no heed. Until a new batch of cowboys came in and pushed their way noisily and roughly towards the bar. And it was at the bar that the altercation began, and spread quickly, though the trio at their little table were never to learn how it actually started. But somebody hit somebody, and somebody hit somebody else, and men shouted and women screamed and somebody called for 'Order' but wasn't heeded at all.

The three hard-bitten phlegmatic men ignored the disturbance until a big feller barged into Delly and knocked the somewhat cantankerous shotgun guard's full shot glass of rye out of his hand, slopping the pungent liquor over the table. Delly immediately rose and gave the man a cuff around the ear which precipitated him most forcibly back into the crowd. But the big feller had a smaller friend who upped and kicked Delly in the knee-cap.

Delly yelped and clutched at the bruised member and hopped on one leg and knocked his own chair over, which got tangled in the smaller man's feet and brought him down also. But by this time the little feller's big friend was on his feet again and tried to kick Delly in the face.

Amos, who was nearest, hit the big feller with a swinging blow to the side of the jaw and down he went again, was spotted a little later crawling away.

But the general battle had reached the trio's table now and they seemed to be surrounded by yelling, threatening faces. This might be the notorious lawman-killer called Amos but he sure as hell couldn't use his shooter in this mill!

Not that he seemed inclined to do so, grinning with pure delight as he shouldered himself away from the table. And soon he and Jangles and Delly were side by side, slugging away at anybody who seemed at all to take umbrage at their presence. And there seemed to be a lot of folk doing that now. Taking umbrage at everything and everybody, breaking heads, jaws, arms, furniture with wild abandon. There was a lot of cursing and shouting and screeching and yippee-ing. Folk were enjoying themselves. And Amos, Jangles and Delly were, it seemed, three of those folk.

Amos blocked a man who tried to brain him with a bottle, winced as he caught the hard glass on his left elbow, drove his right fist into the man's gut and doubled him, kneed him in the chin as he sagged. But that didn't do the fighting marshal's knee much good either and he hopped and swore. A blow from somewhere buffeted his shoulder and he spun on one leg. But the jostling crowd held him up and he was part of it.

'Hello, pard,' nearby Jangles greeted him, parrying a blow from a thin, redheaded cuss, hitting him in the mouth, sending him bouncing. But another man screamed as he was engulfed beneath stamping feet. There was merriment even. But there was a lot of ugliness now also.

Delly was wrestling with a bearded man and they seemed to be dancing, both showing their teeth as if they were enjoying themselves no end. They disappeared, still dancing. But Delly's partner, Jangles, was now back to back with Amos and they met newcomers on all sides. Until Jangles, looking up, yelled, 'There's Rube!'

The stocky man was on the stairs with the brassy-haired filly and was being attacked by two men while the frail stood behind him with her fingers in her mouth. She didn't look all that scared however, just kind of interested.

Rube feinted, struck. A man came over the balustrade and crashed onto a table below, all arms and legs among the crowd, then disappearing. The watching Jangles opened his mouth as if to cheer but this was stopped by a fist and he only managed an agonized yelp as he was knocked down among the feet and the sweaty pants. His bursted lips bleeding, he was hauled upwards by Amos and they were both carried along by the press. There seemed hardly room to swing fists anymore. Men were shoulder to shoulder and belly to belly, wrestling, pushing, grunting, cursing, with now and then a wild shout.

Jangles and Amos were held upright and, neither of them being short men, were able to look over the heads of some of the crowd.

'There's Delly,' said Jangles, spitting blood. The pugnacious shotgun man was ploughing his way towards them.

Amos spotted Rube again. The stocky man was still on the stairs but making his way down now, driving two other men before him as if they were a pair of sheep. His brassy-haired girlfriend was still behind him and looked as if she wouldn't mind joining in the fury herself if she could just get past the fighting deputy.

Groups of battlers milled and slugged. It was a scattered battle and some of it was spreading outside. Amos and Jangles and Delly, close together now, found themselves being carried out back by the press of bodies wherein which they struggled. Soon they were out in the fresh air and, although it wasn't a cold night, after the smoky, sweaty fug in the bar-room that air was like wine. Men were reeling from the effects of it, and some of them, staggering, looked also as if they had been recently worried by wild dogs.

A tall feller with a walrus moustache and a gash in his forehead made a put at Amos, who pushed him away to go down on his butt against the wall; and Amos and his two friends were pushed away from there by the press behind them.

Jangles was wrestling with a cowboy whose pants were in danger of coming down round his ankles and suddenly they were holding onto each other and laughing like loons in the night, mingling their blood. Delly was still looking about him belligerently. He was asking for it. And he was suddenly charged head-on by a feller who looked like a juvenile bull-buffalo and acted that way also.

The tussle carried the two men over to the leaning, pockmarked and ramshackle wooden privy. Jangles and his sparring partner, still laughing, hugging each other like long-lost brothers, followed on, and Amos brought up the rear. Jangles' cowboy friend had managed to get his pants up and cinch them. Jangles' jib looked as if it had been dipped in red paint, and the cowboy didn't look much better. Jangles was calling him by his Christian name, which appeared to be 'Bill'.

Out here, it seemed, nobody was doing much

Legend of Amos

actual fighting now, just swopping insults, staggering, lolling about, sitting down. Except for Delly and his young-buffalo opponent that is, who were still slugging like mad.

Delly got in a wild haymaker and the other gink staggered backwards as if he had been kicked by a fractious mule. He hit the walls of the leaning privy mighty hard and they leaned further, began to crumple. Then they gave way altogether, grinding, moving slowly, then faster, taking the man with them while a glorious shout went up from the watchers.

And this changed to even more glorious laughter, a welcome hilarious sound, as it was seen that the privy had an occupant, bedraggled, half-dressed, ludicrously indignant. But what was even funnier was that Delly, carried by the momentum of his powerful blow, followed his opponent hoppity-skip. And the three men, kicking and struggling, were in the middle of the odorous pile of timber, the dust rising while the hilarity around them reached hysterical proportions.

Jangles and Amos held onto each other and bawled with merriment and the young cowboy was almost helpless between them until Amos staggered away and came to rest in a seated position against an upturned barrel, laughing till tears ran down his aching face.

It seemed like pictures flashed before his mind in the night. He hadn't been in a mill like this, or even seen one, for a long time. It had been worthy of any of the old roaring times (hell, it made him feel young again!), of the battle in Widow's Hole (oh, mercy, poor long-gone Perce Rewberry, husband of Stella, had been in that one), of Jack Rooney's Fight-to-a-Finish Brigade, of Hardneck Gordino, Tall Lincrane, Pack Jack, Big Malcolm; of English Peter and the battle of the Brazos; of Big Rafe, the Spoon Tail and Carolina Walker ... so many hard places and hard men ... so many faces through the years ... so full and fast a life ...

There had been that semi-comical border gang calling themselves the *Diabolica Muchachos*. There had been Dakota Phil and the Kansas Duck, the O'Gonzales band and the Billet Gang ...

The night swirled around him, full only now of un-quarrelling voices, and even laughter. It came to his half-consciousness that the law was now around, somewhat belatedly. There were plenty of cuts and bruises and a few nastier wounds but nobody had died. Men could take a lot and still survive, live to tell the tale as Amos had.*

A man could be a loner. But it was not good for a man to be truly alone. Amos did not think he had ever been truly alone.

There had been deputies. And there had been many others who had helped. *Deputies*. The tragic Perce Rewberry; Parley Masters (where was Parley now?); Manuel the Indian; the New Yorker. And now he had young Rad Spink, and of course, Rube, who had come with him on this trip. A handy man, Rube, and a bit of a card.

Come to think of it, where in hell was Rube now?

Last Amos had seen of him he had been sort of escorting a lady down some stairs, and fighting off all opposition on the way.

Amos hauled himself to his feet, completely

---

* See *Amos Lives!* (and others)

aware now of what was going on around him. And it wasn't bad. He certainly felt as if he had been in a fight, and further inspection of his anatomy was called for. But he didn't think he was going to fall over.

Rube came through the back door in the yellow light which streamed from that source. He walked all right, if rather lopsidedly. Amos joined him and they exchanged notes. Then Rube said, 'That little filly, Amos, she said she'd look after me tonight. Soothe my hurts an' all.'

'I'll bet!'

'Are you goin' back to Golden Bluffs in the morning?'

'I am.'

'I've decided I don't want to stay in Polesen. Do you mind if I ride back with you?'

'Not at all, Rube, be glad o' your company.'

10

Young Molly was out of bed and downstairs and with only a plaster on her head now in place of the white bandage. Her mother, Stella, had thrown a little party to celebrate. Present were the store-folk, Molly and Stella's good friends Harriet and Benjy Kalen; Deputy Rad Spink and his girl Lila; and Rad's old friend Rollo Green and his girl Sadie.

Molly and Stella would both have liked Amos to be there, but they didn't know how long he would be away on his trip to Polesen. They tried not to be too anxious about him.

After a goodly repast they were in the process of sampling the large fancy cake that Stella had baked for the occasion when heavy footsteps were heard in the passage and then the dining-room door opened and two male individuals strode in.

There were cries from the folks around the table. Surprised. Pleased. But a little doubtful. Doubt that was put into words when Deputy Rad asked, 'What in tarnation happened to you two?'

In truth, though Amos and Rube had spruced themselves up before leaving Polesen and hadn't pushed too hard on the trail in the early morning, they still bore signs of that grand bar-room battle. As Rube explained in few words, 'We got in a sort of an argument, but nobody got kilt.'

'Not so far as we know,' said Amos. He grinned lopsidedly. He had a swollen jaw. They both seemed to have swollen jaws. There didn't seem to be much more that could be said about that.

Stella remarked brightly, 'There's still plenty of food left. Come and tuck in.'

'We'll go an' freshen up first,' said Amos.

'Yeh,' said Rube, his eyes on the food.

Molly leapt from the table and ran to Amos, who swept her up, said, 'You look fine, poppet, just fine.' He put her down and, although she didn't know Rube at all well, she hugged him too.

Amos winked at Deputy Rad. 'Operation completed, leftenant,' he said.

'Good.'

The two men left the room but soon returned,

looking sprucer but still somewhat bruised and worn. Hungry, too, after their ride, their horses already tucking in back at the livery stables. Nobody shot questions at the two men now. Swollen jaws or no swollen jaws, they could still chew it seemed, wincing in unison, attacking the food with commendable courage and tenacity.

Whalebone was enjoying himself in Santa Fe. But spasmodically, his mind not easy all the time. He was not a worrying man. But he was an impatient one. To say that he, a thieving killer, was also a conventional man, would have seemed to speak a mockery. But in some ways he *was* a conventional man. Also a vengeful, *clannish* one.

There was something he had to do. He had to do it for himself. And he had to do it for his clan. There was no clan left – except for the two in jail, way out of his reach now – the thought kept coming back, hitting him harder and harder all the time.

Cornelia was good to him. She always was. But now it wasn't enough. He was mighty short with her. And she asked him what was eating him. He wouldn't even tell her. It was his business and his alone, something he had to do.

He knew that Cornelia was concerned for him, had a soft spot for him which she never revealed to anybody else, except maybe to her dark, pretty little companion and factotum, Lola. And Lola was always glad to see him. She never seemed to have anything to do with the men who came and went, as far as Whalebone knew anyway. He'd never noticed anything, and he was the sort who didn't miss much. Neither did Cornelia – have anything to do with anybody else that is, as far as he knew.

Hell, if she did that while he was around ...

But everybody knew that Cornelia was Whalebone's woman, and nobody but an idiot or a visitor from another planet who didn't have his head on right would risk messing with Whalebone's woman while he was around.

Maybe she had secret favourites while he wasn't around. But Whalebone didn't worry his head about this possibility, considering that you couldn't trust any woman while your back was turned. He didn't own Cornelia, and she didn't own him, if lately she seemed to be behaving that way.

Bedevilled by her questions and her possessiveness, he waited till she was away overnight visiting a dying friend, a young frail who had been shot by her jealous gambler lover, and he made a play for Lola. She welcomed him to her bed, but they didn't get up early enough and Cornelia caught them together.

Whalebone had seen two frails fight before but never in a crowded and frilly bedroom. He got out of there.

He was all set to leave. Then he thought, nobody's gonna say I ran out because of women-trouble. So he went back. Lola was nowhere to be seen. But Cornelia came at him like a virago and he knocked her sprawling, semiconscious. She was groaning and mumbling to herself, her face a mess, when he left her again.

I'll take a pasear, he thought. Out of town. Way out of town. I'll come back if I want to, but if I don't want to I won't.

He remembered how only a little while back he had slugged Ma Doombend. Aggravatin' varmints, wimmen! And he was getting well on the wrong side of some of 'em lately. He should worry! Pains in the ass, all of 'em. To hell with 'em!

Back in Golden Bluffs, Rube said, 'Do you think he'll come back then, Amos? Whalebone, I mean.'

'I think he'll figure he has to,' said Amos. 'That's the kind of character he is, an' I ain't aiming to sell him short.'

'So if he comes to town?' Rube seemed to want an answer for everything.

'If he comes peaceable I can't touch him. Like I've said before, I've got no dodger on him and neither has anybody else, far's I know. I'll wait. He'll wait. That's all there is to it.'

'Yeh,' said Rube.

Deputy Rad and his friend Rollo Green, there on the sidewalk in front of the law office with the two older men, didn't have much to say. They hadn't shared in what had happened to those two back in Polesen.

'I'm going down to the Street Place to see Latten, the barman,' said Amos. 'I'm told he's fit enough to be back at his post again.'

'I'll come with you,' said Rube.

The other two watched the short man and the long man going down the street. They both limped, but on different sides, swaying away from each other as if they had suddenly fallen out about something. Green began to laugh.

'What's so goddam funny?' said Rad Spinks.

11

It had been a long time since Lola was alone and on the streets. She had only been a tad when Cornelia picked her up and took her under the wing of herself and her establishment. Cornelia had treated her good, had treated her special. But Cornelia was a woman who could be a powerful hater.

Here in Santa Fe, Lola didn't know where to go now. And it would soon be dark. Luckily she had been able to bring her reticule out with her so she had some money. But she didn't have anything else but the clothes she stood up in. Folks spoke to her. Mostly men. Some of them she had seen before, in Cornelia's place. Not friends. She had to avoid them, turn up her nose at the suggestions. All of them wanted to take her somewhere. What friends did she have apart from the girls in Cornelia's place? And many of those were jealous of her.

She decided to go to Oatsville, the settlement that was virtually owned by the old man called Jika who was a distant relative of hers, a sort of uncle.

On the edge of Santa Fe she had a frugal meal at a small wayside cafe where nobody bothered her and then she went to the livery stables next door and, using up almost all of the rest of her money,

Legend of Amos

bought a gig and a little trotting-horse.

By this time it was full dark and she was scared. But she forced herself to drive out on the dark trail and she set the little trotter at a steady pace and the night wind invigorated her and the road was empty and she became less afraid, almost expectant of what she might find ahead.

It was in the small hours when she reached Oatsville, but a few lights still twinkled there. At the first building, a leaning shack, a man met her on the trail, a horse-pistol in his hand looking as big as a miniature cannon.

'I want to see Jika,' she said boldly. 'I am his niece.' That wasn't strictly true, but it served. The man, his gun hanging at his side, led the way to the biggest building but this only a ramshackle frame-house of no great shakes. The glow of light burgeoned there and the man let her in and called, 'A young lady to see you, *jefe*.'

The fat, swarthy old man sat at the table facing the door. Seated opposite Jika with his back to the door and at the other side of the table, was a tall man, upright in his chair, the lamplight shining on his long, almost golden hair.

Lola gave a little sighing exclamation, for there was no mistaking that long hair and the pose of this man.

Whalebone turned his head slowly. 'Lola,' he said.

It was just a coincidence, and not a very outlandish one, but to Lola it seemed like the answer to a prayer.

Whalebone hadn't had any great plans. He had just been riding. A longish pasear. He had finished up in Oatsville. He knew that Oatsville was where Amos had picked up Cale and Jodie. But he didn't blame boss-man Jika for that. Jika wouldn't take the blame for anything, that was his philosophy and Whalebone respected it. Besides, Jika had been of use to him before – for a price of course – and might be again.

The sudden appearance of the delectable Lola would make the night. Yessir!

And Jika as usual was beaming like the story-book Cheshire Cat.

'Come in, *chiquita*,' he said.

She didn't stay long and, when she left, she left with Whalebone, after Jika had told a minion from outside to direct them to a cabin which just happened to be empty. To call it a cabin, though, was being a little too grandiose. Backing onto a small hill and made up for the most part of wattle and badly-cut logs it was no more than a soddie. It wasn't very clean and it wasn't very fragrant but it did contain a table, a couple of chairs and a cot big enough for two.

The pervading smell seemed to emanate from the cot and Lola said immediately, 'I want new bedclothes.'

'I weel get some, *señorita*,' said Jika's peon and he scuttled away.

They stood in the fresh night air till he returned pretty soon, bringing blankets and pillows which, though well-worn, were clean and smelled of soap. The offending bedclothes were taken away but Lola said the place still smelled.

'I can't smell anything now,' said Whalebone, holding the hurricane lantern that their guide had left with them.

'I have some scent in here,' said Lola, delving in

her reticule.

'That'll give me a splittin' headache,' said Whalebone.

'A big *caballero* like you,' she scoffed and began to sprinkle the stuff around from the little green bottle.

'*Phew-eee!*' exclaimed her swain.

But he didn't object to joining her in the cot when, her olive skin gleaming in the light from the lantern he had hung on the wall, she beckoned to him.

'It's gone kinda chilly,' he said, shivering in his long johns. But she brooked no excuses, only asking him to blow out the lamp, which he did, while she murmured half-jocular admirations at him in Spanish, her fingers busy, peeling, probing.

The girl called Fat Sukie who had her abode in Oatsville was the one who had entertained Cale and Jodie when they visited the settlement. The fat girl had souvenirs of that visit in dying bruises, and a gap in her mouth where one of her teeth had been knocked out. One of them had hit her in the mouth while his partner was doing other things to her, and by that time she hadn't been sure which was which, who was who.

Marshal Amos had taken care of those two and Sukie hoped that they would subsequently hang. But she still carried a hate with her. She knew that Cale and Jodie had been part of Whalebone's clan. And now here was Whalebone himself, large as life, the pretty, long-haired, straight-up, fancy son-bitch! And with that pretty little *puta* who claimed to be kin to Boss Jika.

Sukie liked Boss Jika. Both being fat – and Jika

was inclined to favour women who looked a bit like himself – they had had some times together in the past. But Jika never played favourites for long. Then that *puta* called Lola came along, with Whalebone. And Jika gave the pair a cabin for their ownselves. Fat Sukie had coveted that cabin, mundane though it was. It was certainly better than the noisy, tumbledown frame-shack that she shared with two other girls who, not being large themselves, were wont to sneer at Sukie for taking up too much space.

So Sukie, who hated Whalebone on principle, began to hate his girl Lola almost as much. And she knew where Lola came from.

Sukie did some more figuring. Then she decided to take a little trip.

Although she was big, she was a good horsewoman and often borrowed a large, rawboned mare – they favoured each other – from the local stables.

On this mare she rode to Santa Fe and presented herself at the establishment run by Cornelia Dallahan and to that lady herself.

She did herself some good then, did Fat Sukie. There were gents who preferred fat ladies, Cornelia said, and if Sukie wanted to stay, well ...

Well, well!

Fat Sukie stayed.

And on the following day Cornelia Dallahan had two more visitors, though these were by arrangement. She had sent out a messenger to contact them and, sensing rich pickings (hell, that madam was a mighty rich lady 'twas said) they came post-haste. Two male individuals, youngish but not too young, no kids, something very mean-looking and hard-bitten about them both.

Legend of Amos

The money that Madam Cornelia mentioned made their eyes light up, except that one of them, the tall thin one, had a wall eye and that didn't light up much. His companion, with no neck and a prize-fighter's nose, had eyes like balls of candy and now they looked as if they had been sucked.

'I want both of them dead,' said Cornelia. 'And I want a hank of hair from each of them. Don't try and snow me, boys – I'll know that hair.'

'We wouldn't try anything like that, Miss Cornelia,' said the wall-eyed one in injured tones. 'You know we've got a good reputation.'

'All right. Do it and do it good.'

As they rode out of Santa Fe the wall-eyed one said to the bullish one, 'I wonder why she wants them two dead.'

'Use your gumption f'Chrissakes. Whalebone's been Cornelia's old man for many a year. And the little Mex *tamale* was her favourite too, her bed-warmer.'

'Yeh, well, it ain't gona be easy.'

'It never is,' grumbled the wall-eyed one. But then he neighed with laughter. Then he said, spluttering, 'Hell, this is the best-paid chore we ever had. Let's get it done, an' done with.'

'That's a powerful hating sort of lady,' said the bully-boy.

'Yeh, pardner. An' we should thank our stars she just wants hanks of hair an' not the whole heads like the Apaches an' *mestizos* and Comancheros like to see.'

12

The Street Place Saloon was right in the middle of Golden Bluffs, halfway along the main street with only a hop, skip an' a jump between it and the law office, which pleased the resident marshal no end. When Amos wasn't involved in other business of a more pressing nature, he liked to drink with his friends.

Three of them at this time. Deputy Rad Spink, surrogate deputy Rube, and Rad's friend Rollo Green who, it seemed, wanted to be a deputy too. Amos said he'd think about it. Green was a wild boy who appeared to have settled down. A sweetheart here in town and a planned hitch, and a job at a ranch outside town. But Green said he'd prefer law dogging to bulldogging stupid beef. Besides, there wasn't room for a married couple out at the ranch and Sadie and him would be better in town, the town where they had both been born and raised, the town to which Green had returned after a wide pasear chasing other things which, he said, had led him no-place.

At the get-together at Stella's place Amos had got the idea that Green's girl, Sadie, was in two minds about her prospective spouse changing his profession. Cowpunching could become dangerous at times, but it wasn't half as dangerous as carrying a gun for the law. And there was a rumour going around that although right now Golden Bluffs was halfway peaceable, it wasn't going to last, not as long as Amos stayed at his post anyway. He had given no hint of handing in his badge and so far nobody had asked him to ...

They were bellied up to the bar, all four of them, with one foot apiece on the brass rail, and having a drink with them was the burly barman called Latten, he who'd been shot by Cale or Jodie, whichever, and had been struggling for life for a time but had survived.

His wounded chest was still strapped up and he moved with gingerly stiffness. Temporarily, his wife, plain and plump, half-Comanche half-Dutch, was helping him behind the bar. She it was who had kept him alive, he said, and nobody gainsaid this. She was a mighty respected woman.

Benjy Kalen joined the quartet and now there was sort of a cross-section of ages. Old Benjy and his wife Harriet had run the general stores on the main street as long as redheaded Deputy Rad and his friend, Green, could remember. In Golden Bluffs there had been trouble, though less of it after Amos had become marshal and none for a long time till Cale and Jodie happened along. But, anyway, trouble had come and trouble had gone but folks like Harriet and Benjy went on forever. Like the old doc and the undertaker and the old swamper and his old dog ...

At the moment the old swamper was nowhere to be seen, but his old dog lay in a corner asleep, a *snoring* dog, and the oldest dog that anybody in Golden Bluffs had ever seen.

There was an old Injun too, who actually *claimed* to be the oldest Injun in the territory. He had been sitting in the sun with his back against the wall of the saloon when the marshal and his friends had approached it.

There was an old Mexican lady who lived with her family on the edge of town and she claimed to be even more ancient than the Injun, who didn't know *exactly* how old he was anyway. There were bets laid about which of the two of 'em would die first and, of course, nobody had collected yet. The present favourite was the old Injun, who went by the name of Lazy (and it sure as hell suited him!) and lay in the sun like a lizard most of the time and seemed to draw sunshine into his leathery frame like it was life itself.

Yes, Golden Bluffs was an old town as Western townships went and it had a sizeable share of old folk and, right now, it was a peaceable town again. And in the saloon called The Street Place sunlight shafted and the old dog snored and the murmur of voices and the clink of glasses was a somnolent thread, and for a convivial and resting and drinking man there wasn't a better place to be.

Then, in reluctant tones, Green said, 'Well, I guess I'd better be gtting back to the ranch.'

'Yeh, I guess you'd better at that,' said Rad Spink in mock severity. 'Or the old man 'ull think you've left already.'

Green grinned in his devil-may-care way. 'Yeh, and I wouldn't want to get canned before I decide to quit, that wouldn't suit my book at all.' He was a man who did things that suited his book. What suited his book now it seemed was wanting to be a lawman. And then he would quit being a cowboy.

Amos gave him a sardonic look. He knew that the boy respected him, looked up to him even. But that wasn't all that was needed to make him a good lawman: just the fact that he respected his senior, his mentor, his superior.

Amos had told Rad that he would think about Green as a deputy, and that he would. Hell, he had been a wild kid himself once – a lot wilder than Rad for instance – and he had straightened out.

And Rube aimed to stay in Golden Bluffs also and Rube had already proved himself to be a good man in a pinch, trustworthy, reliable and tough.

Hell, if that officious dead-beat who claimed to be marshal of Polesen – *and was!* – could have a slew of deputies – or 'constables' as the feller insisted on calling 'em – why shouldn't the marshal of Golden Bluffs have more, smaller town though it was?

Now, don't get petulant, old hoss, Amos told himself.

And Rad said, 'I'll ride a-ways with you, Rollo. That all right, Amos?'

'Sure, Rad, no sweat.'

Rube said, 'Amos has got me with him if we have to go out an' catch any stray dogs or anything like that.'

'I don't even feel like going out an' catching me a leetle dawg,' said Amos. 'Fill 'em up again, bartender mine, an' one for yourself.'

'Sure, marshal!'

Big Latten poured gently. At the other end of the bar his wife had her own special bottle of bourbon. No Injun firewater for her! She sipped daintily from a wine-glass, stem and all, and chased and elegant, the only glass of its kind in the place.

A fashion-plate she was not, but a lady she certainly was, yes indeedy!

Spink and Green, both declining another drink, took their leave.

Looked like they were both thinking of really settling down. Not that young Rad had done much else. Born and raised in the town, still going with his childhood sweetheart and planning to marry her. A pillar of the community and a lawman to boot, a trusted deputy. Yes, Amos would trust him with his life! A marshal in the making when the other marshal stepped down. And there was a thought!

Amos knew that Stella wanted him to stay with her. But he knew that she would also want him to hand in his badge. Her husband, Perce Rewberry, who had been younger than Amos, had been a lawman. God, Perce had died young, died on the street like a dog ...

But would handing in the badge solve anything, stop anything? The man who had worn it would still be Amos, the notorious one who in the borderlands had been known as Black Amos. And he wasn't too far from the borderlands now. There were folks who owed Amos nothing but bullets. And one of those folks in particular might turn up at any time now. Here in this saloon even. To shatter this peace. No man could just walk away from that.

He knocked back his drink. 'I'm gonna take myself a little pasear,' he said.

'Mind if I come along, Amos?' Rube asked.

There was only a small pause, and then the lean man with the slash of black moustache looked at the blocky man beside him and said, 'No, not at all, pardner. Maybe this town needs more'n one dog-catcher, huh? Or two or three.'

'Yeh,' said Rube, certainly not the sort for any kind of soul-searching, or even any doubts it seemed. He swallowed his drink and they said so-long to Latten and his missus and a few other folk and strolled out into the sunlit street.

'That Injun,' said Rube. 'He shore can sleep.'

13

But the *sleepiness* didn't last, not even with the ancient Indian called Lazy. Late that night Green and another cowboy from the same spread rode in. The law hadn't expected to see Green again for a day or so. Earlier, Deputy Rad had returned alone after seeing Green home, as Rad put it.

Rad was off duty now and when Green knocked on the door of the law office it was Amos who appeared, and with him was Rube, who seemed to have been made a temporary deputy – *or something*. At least, he was temporarily bunking down in an empty cell.

Green and his friend had a third horse with them and on it was a long bundle covered with a bloodstained tarp.

The second man stayed on his horse and peered nervously into the light streaming from the law office. The third horse stood motionless next to Green's mount, who had nothing in his saddle now. But the burden on the third horse looked a pitiful thing, something that both Amos and Rube had seen before, in the Civil War and since, but not always parcelled and roped.

Green's report was succinct. 'Coupla night-riders tried to run off our hosses. Billy there,' he jerked a thumb in the direction of his mounted companion, 'had just come in from night herding and was putting his nag back with the remuda. The two hoss-thieves spotted him, took a shot at him, but he was in the shadows an' they missed. He returned the fire an' he hit one of 'em. The other one skedaddled, not managing to take even a single hoss. And now we've got an extra one ourselves. He was near his master who was lying there dead as a skunk.'

Green lowered his voice. 'I persuaded Billy to come in, felt he ought to. He's kinda shaky though. He ain't ever shot at a man afore, let alone hit one, deaded him too. I guess it was kind of a lucky shot, the way it hit …'

'No blame will attach to him,' Amos put in. 'Let's take a look at that corpse. Anybody recognize it?'

'Nope. And you'll see why anyway. Best not have it inside, making a mess for you, best have it out here in the light.'

'All right.'

Green went back to his friend, who dismounted. Between them they got the swathed corpse down from the horse, who sniffed at the bundle but didn't move much. They dumped it on the boardwalk and the cowboy called Billy, who seemed little more than a boy, began to fumble with the rope.

Green shouldered him to one side and with a

Legend of Amos

knife whipped from the back of his own belt slashed the rawhide. The tarp seemed to spring apart of its own volition and Billy, straightening, backed away a little.

'Jesus!' said Rube.

'See what I mean?' said Green. 'Nobody could identify *that!* Billy has an old Henry long-gun belonged to his paw. A repeatin' loader ...'

'I was carryin' it,' Billy put in.

The corpse had no face. Nobody wanted to look anymore at what was left. Amos said to Billy, 'You got that gun?'

'Yes, suh.' The lad's face was white in the light, bedewed with sweat.

'Get it, will you, please?'

'Yes, suh.' Billy seemed to get a hold of himself. He was a handsome boy with a firm chin. He went back to the horse and got the rifle and brought it to the marshal who fingered it with appreciation. It was old all right. But it had obviously been looked after with loving care over the years.

'I haven't seen one like this in a coon's age.'

'Me neither,' said Rube.

'An old sixties model,' said Amos, weighing it gently in his hands, the light from the law office burnishing its metal and its well-worn wood. 'Can you still get the original rimfire cartridges for this model, Billy?'

'My paw left a lot.'

'Your paw still around?'

'No, suh, he died.'

'I'm sorry.'

Green said, 'Mistuh Jakeson still sells them cartridges.'

'Do tell.' Jakeson was the local gunsmith.

Something of a collector too.

Green went on, 'Hell, I've been trying to get Billy to sell me that gun – offered him a good price too – for a hell of a long time. Now he's got it blooded I guess he'll never sell it.'

Billy glared at his friend. And Amos said, 'Can it, Green.'

'Sure, marshal, suh.' Unperturbed, he went on, 'Nothing on the body to identify this jasper. No clues.' Already it seemed he had been behaving like a lawman. 'He's young as you can see, an' lean. Look at his duds though, ragged, stinkin'. Looks like a saddle-tramp.'

'Yeh.'

'And the hoss. No brand. No nothing. And I guess this jasper's pard could be in another state now for all we know. Didn't seem much use chasin' him, he'd got too much of a start all on his lonesome, didn't get a thing.'

'Yeh.' Amos turned to Rube. 'Go get the undertaker. Tell him he'll need some help.'

'Right, Amos.' Rube rolled away on his short legs.

A few folk were gathering. Barflies and gamblers and the like, some of whom seemed to stay up all night.

'Move along there,' said the marshal automatically and, desultorily, they did so.

Rube returned with the undertaker who wore dark-grey linsey pants, a brown woollen dressing-gown and moccasins. He was plump and perspiring and accompanied by his assistant, in pants, shirt and stockinged feet, a lank-haired cretinous youth who seemed to have a penchant for this kind of work and handled corpses with loving care. The

Legend of Amos

older man winced. He liked his corpses in better condition than this. 'I can't do much with the face, marshal,' he said.

'Bury him,' said Amos brusquely. 'I'll cover it.'

'I want to do that,' said the young cowboy who had shot the saddle-tramp and would-be horse-thief, and he sounded determined.

'All right, Billy,' said Amos.

Ma was out with the storm-lantern, shielding it discreetly with a fold of a smelly dressing-gown which one of the girls had left, in a hurry after falling out of favour with one of the brothers or cousins.

'It's me, Ma,' a voice called. The figure of the lone rider and his horse became clearer in the night.

'That you, Caleb?'

'Yes, Ma.'

'I tho't you went out with Ben. Where is he?'

'He – he ain't comin' back, Ma.'

The scruffy boy on the horse was upon her then, and he reined in and she glared up at him, not bothering to shade the lantern now, raising it in fact so that it shone on his face, making him blink his eyes.

'Whadya mean, he ain't comin' back? Ben wouldn't run out, he loves his family too much.'

'What's going on?' a querulous voice demanded from behind.

It was Ma's husband, old Nat Doombend, half-drunk as usual, bare-footed, staggering.

'It's Caleb. Ben ain't with him.'

'Why should Ben be with him?'

''Cos Ben went out with him, you damn' jackass.'

'All right, gel,' said Nat in injured tones. 'Don't get on your high horse.' He sounded dignified in a way that only a drunk can and Ma was momentarily disconcerted by this. But then she reverted to type and turned on Caleb once more. 'Get off that nag an' come in the house.'

'Yes, Ma.' The boy sounded almost tearful. He dismounted.

A couple more people had appeared in the shadows and Ma rounded on them in turn and snapped, 'Look after this hoss.'

It was a young couple, more segments of the bewildering clan. 'Yes, Ma,' they chorused, trotting dutifully forward. Everybody called her 'Ma'.

She shepherded Caleb into the biggest ramshackle edifice, with Nat, mumbling indignantly to himself, bringing up the rear. She hung the lamp from a hook in a ceiling beam which didn't look too safe. The lamp swung gently, making shifting shadows. Caleb's twisted face looked like that of a gargoyle doll.

'Ben's dead, Ma,' he wailed.

'Dead?' That was all Ma could say. Then, uncharacteristically, she was bereft of further words.

'How did he die?' That, surprisingly, was the father, old Nat Doombend, his red-rimmed, bleary eyes focusing on his son.

'He was shot, Paw.'

'How?' Ma had her voice back. It rose to almost a screech. 'Goddamit! How?'

'We wuz rambling. You know how Ben liked to ramble. An' pick up things on the way as he allus used to say. We seed these hosses an' there didn't seem to be anybody around and they looked a prime bunch an' Ben said we ought to have 'em ... But – but there was a cowhand – we hadn't spotted him. He – he shot Ben –'

'You said he was dead. How'd you know he was dead?'

'His face was gone, Ma. His head. Half his head!'

'Oh, grief,' exclaimed old Nat, from the background now.

'Where was this?' said Ma. 'Where was it?'

'I ain't rightly sure,' wailed Caleb. 'Ben was leading. He was the eldest, y'know, he allus led me. He seemed to know. But I didn't know. And I couldn't get no hosses. And when I seed what had happened to him I rode, I rode! I didn't want it to happen to me. Did I, Ma? *Did I?*'

'No, I guess not.' She slumped heavily into a chair. Nat was already seated the other side of the rickety table and didn't seem to be taking any part in the proceedings any more.

Caleb looked from one to the other of them and began to sob. Tears ran down his unshaven cheeks and into his dirty neckerchief. He was standing. He bent. Then, with a convulsive lunge, he flung himself at his mother's feet and buried his head in her lap.

She patted his head absently. 'Oh, baby, you was always kinda stupid,' she said. 'But you ain't so stupid that you didn't manage to get back. We'll try an' find out ...' She let her words tail off. She turned and looked at her husband. He seemed to have gone to sleep.

She ran her hand over her face. There were no tears. She couldn't remember the last time she had wept. It must have been when she was just a little tad. She winced. Her face was still sore and swollen from the blow that Whalebone had given her the other day. Things were going bad. But they had gone bad before ....

She gave her boy a not so gentle pat on his head and said, 'Get up, Caleb.'

14

Lola and Whalebone were as snug as two hard-shell bugs in their little cabin in Oatsville. Nobody bothered them, least of all the local *jefe*, Jika. Whalebone kept the fat old half-breed as sweet as a prairie nut in all its fulsome, well-polished flavour. The old bastard is getting too fat and lazy for his own good, the tall outlaw thought. Cross his palm with silver and he'll roll over and let you tickle his gut. But one of these days somebody, and it might even be me, will stick a knife in that fat gut and take over Oatsville for his ownself.

Anyway, nobody else messed with Whalebone. They knew better. And Lola and he ate well, drank well, slept well, made love well, and in between times they went a-riding. Even Pizenhead, Whalebone's rawboned and cantankerous silver-grey stallion, seemed to have fallen in love with Lola, kept nudging her gently with his nose.

The first time he had done this Whalebone had yelled in warning and alarm, for such a manoeuvre from the big horse usually presaged an attempt at a bite. But Pizenhead never bit Lola, and he took titbits gently from her fingers.

'Right now he's acting like a bird,' said the tall man peevishly. 'But watch him, honey, surely watch him. He's as changeable as a desert wind.'

In truth, Whalebone was pretty mixed-up himself about his feelings for Lola. Maybe as he got older he was getting more tolerant in his ways, *softer* even. But he couldn't remember any other woman ever affecting him in quite the same way Lola did. Whatever that was! For Chrissakes, was he in love or something?

But he couldn't seem to be able to pull himself away, ready himself for the other thing he – *but surely!* – just had to do.

They went riding a lot, and one day they went further than usual, Whalebone losing much of his wariness. They halted in a glade a long way from Oatsville and there they made love. Then because it was such a good day they decided to ride onwards a little more, vowing though to retrace their steps before dusk as they didn't think they'd been in this particular territory before and they didn't want to get lost.

Whalebone had never worried before about getting lost. This girl was having a peculiar effect on him. But he was content to go along as they were until such a time that he began to feel different. The world would not dry up and blow away and everything with it. Folks would still move around. Folks would wait, even when they didn't know what they were waiting for ...

And on such a balmy day as this it was good to ride in the sun with a cooling breeze on the face as the sun began to wane, and a space all around with trees and gently waving grass and, in the distance, in a sort of blue haze, a range of low hills which neither of them had seen before. But that didn't seem to matter one way or the other anyway.

But then they saw the two riders coming from that direction, who maybe had ridden from the hills, approaching the pair without haste, two cowboys looking for work maybe, unhurried as wandering cowboys would be.

...Approaching the dark, voluptuous little woman on the small cowpony and the tall, very upright man with the hatchet face and the long hair escaping from beneath his hat and glinting dark-golden in the sun ... and the big silver-grey stallion who tossed his head and flared his nostrils, so that its rider said, 'Easy, ol' Pizenhead, you!'

'Who are they?' Lola asked.

'Damned if I know,' said Whalebone. 'But they look harmless and friendly enough.' From the distance all he could make out was that one rider was tall and thin and the other blocky in the saddle. He could not think that anything could menace him now. Pilgrims! Just pilgrims.

'It's them,' exclaimed the tall one with the wall eye.

'Surely looks like it,' said his blocky companion with the prize-fighter's nose.

'Yeh, that's Whalebone all right. Look at him tall in that saddle like he wuz a goddam sojer-boy. Him and his corset.'

'Yeh, that looks like the girl too. I see'd her before.'

'Yeh, that's her. Who else could it be?'

'Yeh, I guess I recognize 'em both. Do either of

them know you?'

'I wouldn't think so.'

'Nor me.'

'So we take 'em.'

'What, right now?'

'Why not? Do you think we'll get a better opportunity?'

'Well, I guess …'

'They're together. If we try an' take 'em in Oatsville we might have to take 'em separate. And, besides, we might be spotted an' that might cause complications …'

'It's easier in the night …'

'Yeh, but then you gotta make the opportunity. That's here for us now, like on a plate, and they look off-guard, even friendly. Besides, they might be leaving Oatsville now, not going back. Hell, they're coming in this direction, ain't they, away from there? What we gonna do, turn around an' foller them? D'you think Whalebone 'ud sit still in the saddle for that?'

'No-oo, I guess not.'

'Give 'em a leetle salute then. Just a little 'un. Then wait till we get closer and then you move when I move, and don't forget that Whalebone is as fast as a skunk.' It was the thin one talking. He was the dominant one, the intelligent one. He was the fastest-moving too. He might be as fast as Whalebone. Faster!

Hell, there was only one of him, the fancy, corseted bastard – and there was two of them, him and his pardner, and if they didn't take this chance when it was offered to them on a plate they sure as hell didn't deserve to gain anything but a billet in Boot Hill.

The blocky man raised his hand and gave a little half-salute. Like a girl waving a bunch of posies, the thin one thought. But Whalebone gave the same sort of salute in return and the pretty girl seemed to kind of incline her pretty dark head. Pity we've got to finish her too, thought the watching man. But Miss Cornelia must be obeyed ...

'Easy,' he said out of the corner of his mouth. 'Wait for me.'

'All right,' said the blocky man.

15

Pilgrims, thought Whalebone. Saddle-tramps. But as they got nearer, he thought, hard ones!

And the thin one was the hardest, the affable grin that broke out on his face now not quite reaching his eyes.

But Whalebone, although he might have thought that the two might try something – with the girl there an' all! – hadn't expected the thin one to move so quickly, without even a 'Howdy'.

And Whalebone yelled a warning at Lola and flung himself sideways in the saddle as he lunged for his gun.

He felt the blow like a powerful punch at his shoulder and his left hand was jerked from the reins and he clutched desperately for the pommel of his saddle, held it, knowing that if he hadn't acted quickly – *but not quickly enough!* – that slug would have drilled his chest.

But his own gun was out now and the two riders were in front of him and he lifted, thumbed the hammer – and the black smoke was in his eyes and the air was full of it and the booming cacophony of the shots. And Lola banged against him so violently that he was knocked from the saddle.

She rolled away from him in the grass and came to rest face-downwards, but he hardly noticed that then. The two men had been fazed by his precipitate plunge to the ground and he was on one knee then, looking up at them. And he raised the gun level, tilted somewhat, the muzzle pointing, the sun catching it so that it looked like a golden finger. A finger that spat fire and hate as its owner thumbed the hammer twice, three times, moving the gun a little with each shot, seeing the men and horses through the powdersmoke. The contorted faces ...

Then he was hit again, this time in the side, and he was punched backwards to the earth and that buffeted him, then it seemed to close over him and he thought, this is it, this is the end. He tried to lift his gun again but he didn't seem to be able to do so and it was as if he had laid himself down to sleep as the darkness closed over him.

He was surprised to feel the sun upon his face. He opened his eyes and he blinked up into the sun. There was a silence. All he could hear was the thrumming of his own blood, and he knew he was losing a lot of it, it was running from him like sticky water.

The sun was not hot now but even so the light was too much for him and he rolled away from it, but then he had to lie still as pain and nausea tore at him. But then the haze cleared, though the pain went on, and he saw the two men. They lay almost side by side and they were still.

He lay still himself and he steeled himself. Beneath him the grass was being dyed red by his blood. He had been hit in the side and in the shoulder and neither of them had been flea-bites. Both bullets might still be in him and if he didn't do something about that they could bring about his demise. If only he could get on his feet! None of the four horses had taken off anyplace. By dint of moving his head slowly he was able to spot each of them, though they were separated. And his own horse was the nearest, looking at him curiously.

'Come on, you,' he said. 'C'mon, you. Pizenhead!'

The stallion turned his head away disdainfully.

'This is no time to play games,' said Whalebone. He wanted to yell at the beast, curse him loudly as he had done so many times before. But he just didn't have the strength.

He moved his body again and he saw Lola, her lovely face turned up to the sun now as if she had managed to roll over before she died. She must have done. And she looked so very dead. The sight of her, strangely, seemed to give him strength. He couldn't leave her lying like that. His old back, that damn' bugbear, was giving him hell too. But he managed to crawl over to Lola. Then he had to rest again, lying near to her, looking at her. She had been hit in the left breast. Her death must have been pretty quick. She couldn't have suffered much. Her eyes were closed and her face was serene. It was as if she had lain herself down to wait for him, the way she had done back in the trees such a short time ago.

He managed to lift her. Then, holding her, he went along on his knees. Cradling her, calling Pizenhead, just calling him 'horse', softly, cajoling. And, curious, the big silver-grey came forward, only sniffed at the girl as, leaning against the beast, Whalebone managed to get her on the front of the saddle. That horse had liked the girl.

The man leaned against the horse. He was near enough now to be able to see the two attackers more clearly. He might have seen them before. He wasn't sure. It wasn't important now.

The thin one had three eyes, all open, the one in the middle widening like a blossoming red flower. One of the other eyes was walled; they were all sightless, staring blindly at the lowering sun.

The burlier man had been hit in the throat and his head had been forced back so you couldn't see his eyes. He looked as if he were wearing a broad red scarf. I knew I'd hit 'em, thought Whalebone, though I didn't rightly see it. *Hell, I hit 'em good!*

He delved into his warbag and found some rags and used them to wad his wounds as best he could, trying to staunch the blood which was turning his clothes to pulp. He knew he couldn't do anything about the other three horses. Maybe they would have some sense and trail along after him. As for the bodies, they could stay and rot – though the predators would be at them before that, and that was for sure!

He managed to get into the saddle. His spine felt like a red-hot burning rod. He held the girl. The horse was facing the wrong way. He managed to turn him around. The cantankerous stallion was being as tractable as an angel.

'Go, boy,' said Whalebone.

He was carried. It was as if he was in a swaying boat. His senses left him ...

When he awoke he was screaming. His body was on fire. He was held. He struggled. His back was aflame. The fire got worse, spread. It was easier to lie still, let himself be held.

He found that he could see something, if only dimly. Strange wavering shapes, there in the air before him, above him.

He was not being held then. He tried to raise himself and the fire engulfed him once more. He was all screamed out, could only make strange whimpering sounds, pleas for surcease. He was held again. One figure at least was nearer, had the semblance of a real, living person. And the hands of this person held him and they were strong but also strangely gentle. 'You're all right now,' a woman's voice said.

That was a laugh. He didn't feel all right. But the fire was going away and the pain was at least halfway bearable. He was glad that the hands still held him. They stopped him threshing. They seemed to soothe him. Now he was only groaning, a small sound at that. 'Take it easy,' the voice said.

It was comparatively easy to keep still now, let himself be held. But the small sounds seemed to come from deep inside him and were not so easy to quell.

He concentrated on the woman, and the shapes of the other two people who were standing behind her. The woman's face became clear. She looked sort of familiar. Not a girl, but still vestiges of an old prettiness. The shape of one of the figures behind her was more familiar, becoming clearer, the rotund bulk of it.

'Jika!' exclaimed Whalebone. His own voice sounded strange, coming from him in pain, as if he was unused to talking, hadn't talked in a long time.

'Hallo, *amigo*,' said the fat man, *jefe* of Oatsville. 'We thought for a while that we'd lost you.'

It all came back then to the man in the bed. He was in a bed after all, not a cloud! 'Lola,' he said.

'We buried her,' Jika said. 'We gave her a good funeral.'

'It was a good funeral,' said the woman and she let go of her patient and straightened up. Just one of Jika's girls. 'Am I in town?' Whalebone asked. There was another man behind Jika, a thin, younger man, one of the chief's hardcases: Whalebone had seen him around, didn't know whether he'd known his name, couldn't remember it anyway, *not important*. 'You're in town all right,' said Jika.

'I got here all right then?'

'Only just. You seemed like dead in the saddle. You and the girl sort of holding yourselves up, two dead ones.'

'Lola was dead.'

'Yeh. So were you – almost.' The fat man rumbled with laughter. 'We almost buried you as well.'

'How long have I been like this?'

'Days. We took two slugs out of you. We thought you were dead then, thought we had wasted our time. But you fooled us. You came round again. And here you are.'

'Here I am,' said Whalebone.

'You was outa your head for a time. Prattling like a loon. Names now and then. Lola o' course. Cornelia. Guess that'd be the madam back in Santa Fe, huh, Cornelia Dallahan?'

'I guess.'

'And Amos. Would that be the feller they used to call Black Amos?'

'I guess.' Whalebone said no more. Jika didn't tell him that he, too, knew Amos, that in fact Amos had been here not so long ago and picked up a couple of prisoners, folks incidentally whose names had been linked with Whalebone. Jika had his spies, his informants. But Jika didn't mess with things that didn't concern him, didn't give out information either unless he was paid for it. He'd make Whalebone pay somehow – hell, he already had Whalebone's poke! – but he didn't feel like giving the man any information. His people had saved the man's life, so, let that be it for the time being.

He asked, 'Did Amos have anything to do with this, do you think?'

Whalebone answered without hesitation. 'No, I don't think so. Not his stripe.' And that was the truth. Cornelia, he thought, it had more the stripe of Cornelia, a jealous, vindictive bitch!

'Who? Do you know? Or were you bushwhacked?'

'No, I saw 'em. Couple of saddle-tramps looking for easy pickings, anything that came along.' That could be the truth after all. But, somehow, Whalebone didn't think so. Sufficient for Jika though. 'I got 'em both. Out by the hills.'

'Do tell.' Jika shrugged massive shoulders. He

Legend of Amos

wasn't about to send out any of his people to pick up such rubbish, which would be part eaten up by now anyway. 'You came a long way with those two slugs in you, *amigo*,' he said.

'I'll go further without 'em,' said Whalebone. 'And as soon as possible. There's somep'n I have to do. I've got to get out of here. *I've just gotta!*'

'It can't be for quite a while yet,' said Jika. 'You've lost a lot of blood. And you didn't have any to spare, skinny thing like yuh. You move too soon and you'll start it all again and then you will kill yourself.'

I guess he's after Amos, the fat man thought, and I guess I know why. But it was none of his never-mind.

'Go to sleep,' the woman said and Whalebone seemed to take heed of her, his eyes closing slowly, ghostlike.

PART THREE

The Killing Trail

16

Eight-year-old Molly Rewberry was as good as new again. But, she affirmed, she was 'more interesting' now. She had a smallish scar, not particularly ugly, in the shape of a bent horseshoe on her left temple. By combing forward a lock of her curly, dark-brown hair she could conceal this. But most of the time she liked to brush her hair back, the way she used to wear it, pigtail and all.

She had had her hair cut and the pigtail was gone. She showed the scar proudly and was the envy of her schoolmates, the boys in particular. None of them had been run down by a desperado on a horse. Jumping cats, he could've shot her, couldn't he?

To top this, Marshal Amos was a sort of uncle of hers, that legendary man who had caught the desperadoes, brought them in, finally handed 'em over to the big law.

The boys would have wanted to see more desperadoes, to see the marshal in action. None of 'em had seen a thing. Only Molly had seen anything – before she'd been put down by that desperado of course.

But, although there were dark rumours about a killer on his way to Golden Bluffs, the days went by and nothing happened and the rumour died and the town went on in its old humdrum way just like it used to, and the boys played cowboys and Injuns, and some of the girls too.

Sometimes boys and girls tried an enactment of Molly's adventure, with Molly as the chief character of course. But even this began to pall, was dropped. And Molly began to let her curly hair fall over her brow and quit bragging. An intelligent child, she realized that enough was enough.

Her mom and Marshal Amos did a lot of horse-riding together. Sometimes she went with them. Other times she stayed with Harriet and Benjy Kalen at the store. Her mom didn't like her to be alone. But then of course there were Amos's deputies, one or the other of them around the house or at the office. Rad and Rube, and sometimes Green who seemed to be a sort of honorary deputy now, although he hadn't yet given up his ranch job.

And then there was Green's girl, Sadie, or Deputy Rad Spink's girl, Lila. Molly was a popular kid. And there were always the boys of course, her schoolmates who vied with each other in walking her to and from the schoolhouse, carrying her bits an' bobs.

Life and sunshine flowed around Molly, who walked as if she were dancing. And everything was good. She was healthy, she was pretty, she was growing up to be a smart young lady. She thought she might train to be a teacher. Her own teacher had said she thought the girl might have a sort of aptitude for this kind of thing. But that would be some time hence.

Molly liked the open air and the sun. Maybe she

Legend of Amos

would marry a rancher's son some day and then have a big ranch. But the only rancher's son she knew was Ben Links, who was about her age and went to the same school. Her friend Rollo Green worked for Ben's dad, who by all accounts wasn't half bad. He had certainly been easy with Green about that young man's deputying. But the old rancher's only son, Ben, was a real pain in the butt and Molly, who could be disconcertingly ribald at times, had more than once told him so.

Molly thought about Uncle Amos and she wondered if there would ever be any lady marshals.

You could imagine all these things. You could pretend to be some of these things. And the days flowed by and in the good times even school could seem like a holiday. Events took place. Prize-givings. A wedding or two. A few fights that were more funny than horrendous, dances, house-raisings, big picnics, horse and foot races, one funeral – and that of an old man who had been sick for years – and nothing, it seemed, to worry *anybody* about *anything*. The undertaker and the law were having it easy and the local medico wasn't overworked and the benevolent goodwives had forgotten the last time they were able to have a good ache-jaw gossip about anything or anybody.

Jika said that Whalebone had the constitution of a young bull-buffalo. And Jika wasn't the sort to be giving out with fulsome compliments. Whalebone had a good nurse. She was no Lola, but she was a comfortable woman. And the lean man seemed to have something that was driving him and when he, to sort of celebrate his new health, made love to the woman, it was violent and long as if he were testing himself to the utmost. And all she had to do afterwards, when he had taken off his corset, was rub his back with liniment.

He had good flesh, she said. His wounds were healed. Now puckered scars were all that remained of them and the man would carry those for the rest of his life.

He began to practise with his gun, and he told the woman he was as good as ever and it was time for him to go. She watched him go. She wondered whether she would ever see him again.

He had not told anybody where he was going.

But he went straight to Santa Fe, only pausing once, bivouacking for a while not far outside that famous town and waiting for darkness before he finished his journey, reached his destination.

He entered Cornelia Dallahan's place by a back way he knew well, although it had been his habit most times to go in the front like a nabob and be treated like one. But there was no Lola to greet him this time and no Cornelia would be coming down the stairs with open arms. He chuckled savagely at the thought of it.

There was a man at the top of the narrow back-stairs and he didn't seem surprised to see Whalebone, just said 'Evenin', suh'. A thickhead bully-boy Whalebone had spotted a few times before. Nobody would tell him anything, least of all his boss, Madam Cornelia!

'Where's Miss Cornelia?' Whalebone asked.

'In her room as far as I know, suh.'

But Whalebone took no chances. He went past the man and then he turned, drawing his gun smoothly. He laid the long steel barrel hard against the back of the bully-boy's head and caught him as he slumped and propped him against the wall in a seated position. The man looked as if he'd be out a long time. If he ever woke up. Walking very lightly, Whalebone went on.

He was on carpeting now and Cornelia's room was right ahead of him at the end of the passage.

He had already reholstered his gun. His hands swung free. He tried the door and found it unlocked. As far as he remembered it had never been locked. Cornelia figured she had plenty of protection. Whalebone opened the door and walked through.

Cornelia had a small sitting-room. One sweeping glance told Whalebone that it was empty. No bully-boy here. One on the stairs, unconscious, unarmed, because his attacker had taken a gun and knife. And two or more downstairs, out of sight, out of earshot unless shouts, screams or gunfire started up. And this was the big girl's bailiwick, away from the rest of them and quiet as a saloon in the early morning. And hell, Cornelia was no 'girl'. She was no lady either, just a jealous, double-crossing murderous bitch!

The bedroom door was slightly open. Whalebone knew that bedroom well. Cornelia always called it her 'boudier'. It was not small though. It was large and it was luxurious and Cornelia spent a lot of time in there, at her desk, or in her favourite overstuffed armchair at the side of the ornate French table which had on it her wine, her special thin cheroots, her box of bon-bons.

She was a beautiful woman. She was a businesswoman and a very successful one in her chosen business and its side ramification. She was a greedy woman in all things and in recent times an increasingly lazy one. There were signs that she would get fat. Whalebone had noticed these signs. I shall have to make sure that she doesn't get fat, he thought with wicked humour.

He catfooted across the smaller room and pushed the second door wider to reveal the much bigger room behind it.

His glance switched to the bed first and that was where he almost outfoxed himself. The bed was empty in its hugeness, made-up, pristine and colourful. Cornelia liked bright colours. Whalebone's eyes caught movement then and he swivelled his head, and his body too with that erect movement he had, fast though, well-practised. And drawing his gun again was part of that movement.

Cornelia was in her armchair, which had been moved, was further away from the bed than it used to be. She wasn't exactly in it, she was on it: between her and the base of the chair, the seat, was a young man, a Fancy Dan, Whalebone thought, little more than a kid, a handsome boy with white teeth bared and wicked eyes.

The boy let go of Cornelia and she slid off his lap and hit the carpeted floor with a small thump. She yelped. But whether it was a cry of alarm at the sight of Whalebone or a yelp of pain would have been hard to determine. She was in her robe and didn't seem to have much on underneath and there was certainly no bustle to break her fall.

The boy was in his shirtsleeves. As she dropped, the woman seemed to forget all about him and she stared at the visitor with eyes that threatened to fall out of her head. Shocked eyes, haunted eyes, eyes then that were full of abysmal fear. Eyes terrible in horror. *And guilt!*

'Yes, I'm still alive, honey,' said Whalebone.

Her lips formed his name but no sound came out.

'But Lola's dead,' he said. 'Still, your boys didn't tell you that, did they? They couldn't.'

Her red lips yammered. 'I,' she began. 'I ...'

And that was when her boyo acted. Throwing himself sideways to his gunbelt on the ornate table, the butt of the gun nearest to him. He was fast too. He had his hand round the butt when Whalebone shot him. Two rapid shots. Making sure. The first one would probably have done it, the one in the side of the head which forced the young man around towards the man with the gun so that the second bullet caught him full in the chest and slammed him flat on his back on the carpet. His wildly-sprawling leg caught the table and tipped it, and wine-glasses and bottle and cigarettes and a box of cheroots and bon-bons were scattered on the floor with the gunbelt, the unused gun.

'Crazy show-off young bastard,' said Whalebone.

Cornelia screamed and went past him and continued to scream. He turned and shot her in the back of the head, slamming her against the bedroom door which, as it had been already ajar, he hadn't bothered to shut behind him. Her bulk shut it fast, but then she slid away from it so that he only had to clamber over her legs in order to get by. Then, without pushing her dead weight out of the way, he was able to get the door wide enough open for him to be able to squeeze his thin frame through it.

There were stairs at each end of the passage and, after passing through the small sitting-room and out through the final door, Whalebone paused momentarily. He heard bootheels on the front stairs, the main ones, and he turned the other way to the back stairs which he had used when he came in.

The bully-boy he had slugged was still against the wall. He had slid a little sideways but there was no sign of movement in him.

Pizenhead the stallion waited out back. He hadn't been getting a great amount of exercise in recent times and was kind of fidgety. He needed no urging to put his best foot forward. They've got to get horses, the man thought, and nobody's gonna catch this one.

17

'A funny thing,' said Rube.

'What's that?' said Amos.

'That sleepin' Injun, the one they call Lazy, I've just been talking to him.'

'And did he talk to you?'

'Yeh.'

'You're highly honoured, bucko.'

'Oh, me an' him, we've got a sort of understanding. I fell over his laig once, you see, an' bruised him a bit. But we smoked the peace pipe.'

'What did it taste like, this pipe?'

'I was just joshing, Amos.'

'I know.'

'That ol' man ain't always as sleepy as folks think he is. He's got his wits about him. He just doesn't cotton to moving about much is all.'

'I never took him for no idiot. So what did you two talk about?'

'It seems that when Green and his friend Billy were bringing in that horse-thief that Billy shot, Lazy took a glance at him an' recognized him. The dead horse-thief, I mean.'

'Hell, that was time gone. Why didn't the old man say somep'n at the time? I ain't aiming to get that thief dug up again so we can have an identification parade. Billy paid for that burying, y'know.'

'I know. I guess ol' Lazy didn't think it was important at the time, him figuring who the horse-thief was, that one being dead and finished an' all.'

'Well, all right. But who did Lazy figure he was then, that horse-thief?'

'He was purty sure it was one of the Doombend boys, that scummy clan that have a little settlement of their own.'

'I heard o' them. Never came across 'em though, far as I know. You know where they're at?'

'No, cain't say I do.'

'Does Lazy know?'

'Didn't say. I can ask him, though, if you want me to.'

'But he wasn't plumb certain sure?'

'Hell, Amos, that corpse had half its face shot away. It was just somep'n about it that made Lazy think …'

'Such as?'

'He didn't say. Hell's bells, I wish I hadn't mentioned it to you now. You're like a ferret with a rabbit's foot. Anyway, if it was one of the Doombend boys we know he only had one other feller with him, an' that could've been anybody an' neither of 'em got away with a thing, 'cept one of 'em ended up dead.'

'You're right,' said Amos with magnaminity. 'But see if you can get more out of Lazy anyway. I'd like to know more about these Doombends, if the old man knows more, y'know. Just as a matter of interest, huh?'

'Yeh,' said Rube. 'Yeh, Amos, I get you. I'll get me some coffee first, though.'

'It's on the stove.'

'Anyway, I guess Lazy's gone back to sleep again by now.'

Whalebone rode hard at first but he took a circuitous route, weaving and winding and doubling like a wolf bitten in the butt by a rabid skunk. But then, not having seen any signs of pursuit, he slowed down, travelling by night, not bivouacking until the sun came up again and he could see around him. He had provisions, smokes, coffee, even a bottle of not very good rye whisky. He lit a small fire in a dip. He even slept a little, and nothing bothered him.

He was nudged awake by the nose of the stallion, Pizenhead, who never needed hitching, had been browsing on the grass nearby.

There was nothing else moving around, so the nudging hadn't been any sort of warning. 'You're kind of impatient, ain't you, you old bastard?' said the man. 'Now you're on the run again an' all. Still, I guess I'm lucky you didn't choose to bite my ear off. All right, let's move again. We can stop for more sustenance a mite later. I'm getting kinda short on water at that. But I know roughly where I'm at now and, unless the earth's swallowed it up, there should be a small crick just ahead.'

He wondered how many miles he had travelled while talking to this big stallion since he had first had him and they had evolved a sort of quarrelsome rapport. It had always been Whalebone's contention that Pizenhead just didn't like people. But Whalebone was the only human who could ride him, and that was certainly something.

They were on their own now and that was the way it should be, Whalebone figured. He felt more comfortable now, less *driven*. He had done part of what he had planned to do. His constitution was good. He could *pace* himself. Getting steadily towards the place of the rest of his plan, the culmination of his *planning*. Not that it had needed much planning. As far as he was concerned it was a foregone thing. Something he had to do. Kill or be killed.

This last part wouldn't be as easy as the other part had been. That had been easier than he had expected in fact. But there would be repercussions, *of course there would*! So he had, but without any too frenetic haste, he had to do the rest of it, the finish of it, before the repercussions became more widespread. And then if he survived it was him for over the border, for Mexico. He didn't mind Mexico too much at all. It was hotter there, good for his back.

*

The rider came straight. It was a feller Rube used to know. He had news. Whalebone had killed two people in Santa Fe. That madam, Cornelia Dallahan, and a young feller she had been sparking of late, feller called Jollo who had been trying to make his name as a pistolero and an all-round hell of a feller. He was a hell of something now all right. But he had had a good funeral. The frails had seen to that when they buried the big boss, their mother hen. The wailing of the wake had been heard for miles around.

Yeh, it had been Whalebone all right, the killer. He had been spotted good. By a bully-boy whose skull he had split, and by others as he left town.

But after that he had sort of disappeared.

But, 'twas said, he had been sort of coming in this direction.

'So the law is after him,' said Marshal Amos. 'If he comes here I've got him, he doesn't need to brace me nohow.'

'*If* he comes here,' said Rube.

'He'll come here,' said Amos.

18

'I remember somep'n, Ma,' said Caleb the Doombend boy, 'about the ranch were Ben was kilt.'

'I've asked you enough times,' the big woman said, 'that you might remember somep'n.'

'It was dark I told you an' things happened so quick. Ben was there – an' then he was gone an' I had to get outa there fast or I'd be gone too, and you wouldn't have seen me again either. But I remember somep'n now, just came to me.'

'Quit pussyfootin' then an' tell me.'

'There's a pool there, a small one but sort of long an' narrow. And on the edge o' this are two privies side by side. I remember Ben saying that it was a funny place to put privies.'

'I'd say it was the ideal place,' commented Ma. 'I'm surprised you didn't remember a thing like that before. Now you've got your damn' wits back do you remember anything else?'

'No-oo. I bin racking my brains. But no.'

'Have you any more idea now then where the place is at?'

'No-oo. I bin racking my brains but …'

'I heard you the first time. Now what you do is, Caleb, you wander around and you tell the other folks an' you ask if anybody knows of a ranch with a pool with a coupla privies beside it. You understand me, boy?'

'Yeh, Ma. Sure, Ma.' Caleb shambled away.

Idiot, thought the big woman. He was her son all right, but she wasn't sure whether Nathaniel was his father or it had been somebody else. Ben had been her son. He hadn't had much sense either, the way he had behaved. Ben shouldn't have died. But if Caleb could find out …

Nat was calling her. He was drunk as usual.

But Caleb caught up with her again about half an hour later and said, 'Lessiter knows where that place is. Says it's not far from a town called Golden Bluffs.'

'I heard o' that,' said Ma. Lessiter was a younker who had wandered in on them a few weeks ago, a price on his head. A murderous young bastard. But certainly sharper than Caleb.

'He said he can take us there,' said Caleb. 'He's raring to go.'

He would be, a hell-raising young wild-man. But useful. 'Well take 'em tonight,' Ma said. 'And we won't come back empty-handed this time, an' we'll mebbe take a few scalps, pay for Ben.'

'Yeh, Ma,' said Caleb, his ugly face beaming.

Ma gently rubbed her face where Whalebone had hit her. It was still swollen a bit and felt kind of tender.

She would welcome some action.

She figured to hit the ranch in the deeps of night. Not too long before dawn but not too near either. The time when nobody would be up, the time when folks slept the deepest before the dawn. She had known marauding Indian bands who struck at that time in the old days. She didn't believe that all Indians were superstitious about fighting by night, although for all she knew some of 'em might be.

Caleb came back and he had lean, mean-featured Lessiter with him and they were both cock-a-hoop.

'Hold your hosses,' said Ma. 'I'll tell you when.'

They hit the ranch about the time Ma had figured. It was a dark night but light enough for what they wanted to do. Lessiter hadn't put a foot wrong, led 'em like a bird-dog. They got plenty of horses. And a ranny came out of what was maybe the bunkhouse and maybe he was making for one of the privies, but he didn't get that far. They all poured lead at him and he shook and fell and lay still.

'All that lead 'ull keep him down,' somebody said as the echoes died. Screaming and yippee-ing, they lit out, and the horses streamed before them. They didn't see anybody afterwards. They had an almighty start.

Ma, after getting her bearings, led them on a different route back. She didn't seem to need Lessiter anymore. She even detoured a bit, saying she knew this territory now. She took them over rocky ground at the base of what one of the men referred to as 'pissy, half-hearted hills'. They were just lumps on the ground. The hooves of the horses left no trace and Ma said it would be a wise old Injun who'd be able to track 'em across here, she didn't think any Injun could be that clever.

They reached their billets without mishap, not a scratch on men nor beasts. It was way past dawn and the sun was coming up.

It was sun-up when the news reached town. It was Green, who had been at the ranch. The boy who'd been killed was a friend of his, so full of holes that he looked like a tattered red doll.

'They got most of the horses,' said Green. 'Lucky mine wasn't in the corral. We weren't able to chase 'em, just saw which way they seemed to go is all.'

It was early. Amos; but no Rad Spink. Rube was there though, and Amos said, 'We'll need a tracker. How about Lazy, Rube?'

'I'll see.'

But the old Indian wasn't yet at his post against the wall of the saloon and Rube had to go looking for him. Finally, he saw Lazy shambling up an alley as if he were coming from someplace, Rube wasn't sure where. He called out. Lazy seemed to hear him but came on at the same slow, hoppity-loppity pace. Then Rube's attention was deflected from the sight of his Indian *compadre*.

Out of the corner of his eye Rube saw a tall man on a big grey horse coming down the middle of main street in the morning sun.

Rube turned himself around and looked straight at the rider. He virtually forgot all about Lazy for a time.

Amos had been at the jail to open up and wake Rube who was sleeping in an empty cell. In fact both of the two cells were empty. Not even a drunk, for which Rube was thankful as he himself slept as quietly as a possum, but deeply too, so that Amos had had to shake him well, saying scornfully, 'A fine guard you'd make.'

'Who needs a guard?'

'You never know,' was the dark rejoinder.

This was before Green turned up with the news from the ranch and Amos sent Rube to look for old Lazy. But then Amos and Green went to Stella Rewberry's place where Amos was expected for breakfast and where he hoped to meet Deputy Rad Spink. Young Molly, just going out to school, hugged Amos and Green in turn. She had lately taken a shine to Green, and Green's girl Sadie had pouted and told Molly how jealous she was, sending the little girl, her old self again, into squeals of delighted laughter.

Amos and his companion saw Molly out of the way before they gave Stella the bad news, neither of them knowing that there was worse to follow.

Stella was outraged. She had friends at the ranch too, had known the young man who had been killed. 'I can only stay for coffee, honey,' said Amos.

'Have a couple of those buttered hotcakes anyway. You too, Rollo.'

'Thank you, ma'am.'

They drank the scalding dark brew and stuffed their mouths with food. Rad didn't turn up and Rollo Green said the feller was probably with his girl, Lila Keene.

The two men, after bidding an anxious Stella goodbye, were on their way to the girl's home when they saw Rad striding towards them.

The shorter, stocky Rube was hopping along at the back, trying to catch up with Rad who didn't seem to have noticed the older deputy. The two men approaching couldn't understand why Rube didn't call out. But the street was still almost empty except for a couple of kids at the other end. Maybe Rube didn't want to wake somebody up. Didn't look as if Rube had found old Lazy, let alone woke him up. Unless the old Indian didn't want to be bothered yet awhile – or ever. He was no warrior. Had he ever been one?

Rube caught up just as Rad reached Amos and Green.

Rube was somewhat out of breath but he managed to say, 'He's here.' He was looking at Amos and Amos asked, 'Who's here?'

'Whalebone. Just got in. Large as life and full of vinegar. He's gone into the hotel for a wash-up.

Says he had himself a sleep and some tucker an' coffee on the trail before he came in ...'

Rube stopped for breath but started up again almost immediately. 'Says as soon as he's clean he'll be ready for you. He's already got his horse fixed. Fine grey stallion ...'

'Get on with it!'

'Says he wants it in the old way, man to man, gun to gun.'

'He'll have it that way then,' said Amos.

He looked at Green and Green said, 'You've just got to do this first, Amos.' Green understood. He was an intelligent and uncompromising young man.

'Somep'n surprised me,' said Rube. 'About Whalebone, I mean.'

'What's that?' asked Amos.

'He's got a sense of humour.'

'Maybe he's gonna need it,' said Amos. 'You boys keep outa this, y'understand?'

They all nodded, unspeaking. They understood.

19

Lessiter was a mighty peeved young man. It was he who had led the Doombends to the ranch with the two privies by the long pool. From there they had collected a prime batch of horseflesh on the hoof and had filled a nosey ranny with so much lead that his friends would be able to bury him without digging a hole with a shovel, could just bounce him up and down on the ground till he sank for good.

Thus Ben Doombend was avenged.

They had flown free like birds, the riderless horses streaming ahead of them as if they were eager to find their new home.

And not a whiff of pursuit all the way.

They were home now, men and beasts.

Old Nat hadn't been out with them of course. To take him along they would've had to tie him in the saddle. Then somebody might have shot him. He had waited for them.

He had got the booze ready for them. One good thing you could say about old Nat, he never ran out of booze. And some of the women had got piping eats ready.

Ma had gone along with the raiding-party, had led them in fact – as most always, Lessiter had been told. That was why she had been so all-fired mad when Caleb and Ben had taken that ranch on their lonesome, just the two of them, and Ben had been killed. Mean-faced Lessiter could well believe what he was told about that big old lady.

His own ma had been a gentle creature. It was his pa who'd been the wrong 'un. He had died at the end of a rope in the hands of a bunch of townies, blazing-eyed vigilantes, after he had been caught robbing a till and had killed a popular storekeeper.

Lessiter took after his pa, but that didn't faze him none. Old lady Doombend should've been *his* ma, he thought. Riding like she had! With him on one side and her son, Caleb, on the other. And, if she looked like a badly-filled sack o' meal when afoot, on a horse with her fine boots she was as good as any male rider an' better than most.

She could shoot too, and Lessiter had already seen her at work with the big knife she sometimes toted, when she carved one of the hangers-on, ripping his arm open from elbow to shoulder because he got out of hand with one of the old lady's numerous 'daughters'.

When the bunch got back from the raid they didn't sleep. Once the new horses were penned, the thieves set in to filling their faces and carousing.

Lessiter had some food and coffee. But he never drank booze because it did things to his guts which weren't nice, he couldn't figure why. Once an old sawbones had told him he must have what the old goat referred to as a 'ticklish stomach'. In earlier days Lessiter had been joshed about this disability of his. But he had a murderous temper. And now he had a murderous reputation, a price on his head for killing a stick-man in a gambling hall in San Antone. The skunk's table had been rigged and Lessiter had told him so.

The croupier had drawn a little Bulldog pocket-pistol and Lessiter had beaten him, shot him between the eyes.

Self-defence, Lessiter had said, and he had witnesses, he should've got a medal for putting down a wiggly snake like that one. But that had cut no ice with the gambling management or the local constable who'd been pocketing their kick-backs.

Lessiter, fast as a cougar when needs be, prickly pear under his tail an' all, had only escaped a posse by the skin of his butt and, after shaking them off, had finished up at the Doombend encampment.

Legend of Amos

Ma asked him no questions, except, in fact, was there a posse on his heels? He said there wasn't, which was the truth by then. Completely venal, and pretty astute also, Ma recognized this younker's stripe and figured she'd be able to use him. And such had happened.

But, now everything was done, it seemed almost as if Lessiter wasn't a member of the 'clan', as of course really he never had been. And young Caleb was crowing – as if it was he who'd been leading the raid on the ranch by the long pool.

Hell's bells, Lessiter thought, that idiot couldn' even find the place. And, if he ever had found it this second time, he would've likely finished up dead like Ben Doombend had on that inept pair's first visit there.

And Lessiter's peeve grew. He fended off the advances of a pretty *mestizo* girl who followed him a-ways. She was too tiny and fragile-looking for his taste anyway. He felt like killing young Caleb, shutting his blabbing loose mouth for good. But he knew that then Ma would have his tripes, and in the most long-winded, painstaking, not to say *painful* manner imaginable.

But Lessiter, completely on his lonesome now, soon had a plan that was a whole lot better and, without more ado, he set this in operation.

He took his time. He chose three of the new horses, the pick of the bunch. Hell, they probably ain't even counted 'em, he thought, they wouldn't miss three of 'em. He hadn't counted them himself, didn't waste time in doing so now.

It was full light now and the sun was getting warm. Already the celebrating thieves and their hangers-on were well into their cups, as rowdy as squabbling roosters. Lessiter had already noted that Ma was no exception, seemed even to be keeping pace with her old man as they knocked back the rotgut hooch.

Lessiter made sure that he had some grub and water just in case he got sidetracked. But he'd already figured to go straight to Oatsville. He figured that old Jika would give him a good price for the three horses, and that old *jefe* seldom asked questions, a fat law unto himself as he was. Jika knew Lessiter.

The young man decided that while he was at Oatsville he would also pay his respects – and more! – to Fat Sukie. Being a bony son of a sea-cook himself, he liked girls with plenty of beef on 'em, and Sukie was one of the primest examples he knew and on top o' that she liked him!

Mounted on his own little paint, Lessiter shepherded the three stolen horses away, and they were as good as trotters out for a spin in the morning sun.

Amos went around the backs of town. He wasn't skulking: nobody on earth could have accused him of that. He was just doing what he had decided to do, just him, not anybody else. This was his job, his go-down on this quiet sunny morning. He did not think about the way the morning would end. He thought that what he meant to do now was the right thing to do. He *knew* it was right. He had never been so sure in his life.

A face appeared at an open kitchen window and the female owner of the face looked a little startled, those eyes wide and the reedy voice exclaiming 'Good mornin', marshal' before the window closed on his reply as he raised his hand to his hat-brim. There was nobody in sight then. He was alone again. And that was the way it should be.

He turned a corner and the sun's rays hit him full in the face so that he had to squint. But here was his first destination. The long, low building with the small bell-tower. He had heard the bell ringing. But it had long since stopped. He had been so used to hearing it that he had hardly noticed it at all this morning, he thought, which was kind of strange.

This was not the church though. This was the school. Not as quiet as the church. A buzz coming now as if from a hive of bees – with an occasional yelp. And the teacher's measured tones. Widow Miz Salmondene, a fine lady who, a trained dominie from way back, had taken up the profession again after the death of her husband who had run a feed-barn on the edge of town.

You could see the feed barn from here, still owned by Miz Salmondene but run for her by her nephew, a strong young feller called Boze.

The door of the schoolhouse was partially open and, as Amos approached in, the bustle of learning came to him like a tide flowing back and forth. It was a stimulating sound, yet a sort of peaceful one also. Amos pushed the door wider and went through but then paused to get his eyes accustomed to the new light, and to the shadows, the bars of sunlight, the brightness and the soft gloom.

A voice said 'Hallo, Uncle Amos' and he realized that young Molly was in a seat near to him. Then other treble voices of both sexes said 'Good mornin', marshal' in a ragged chorus.

'Children!' said a more adult voice in a sharp female timbre. They loved Miz Salmondene. And they respected her too, and they became quiet. And she asked, 'Can I do something for you, marshal?'

'Could I see you outside for a moment, ma'am, if you please?'

'Of course,' she said. He turned about and she followed him out, closing the door behind her, shutting off somewhat the hum, though some of it, strengthening it seemed, came from the open window then.

'Is everybody at school now, Miz Salmondene?' Amos asked. 'Will there be any late-comers, do you know?'

'They are all here, marshal. I have called the register.'

'And they will stay there now till playtime, no outdoor things I mean?'

'Not this morning, marshal. Why, do you think there is some trouble brewing?'

He wondered if she had heard anything. Her serene face, which once must have been very beautiful, told him nothing at all, and he did not ask.

'I think there will be trouble, Miz Salmondene,' he said bluntly, for that was his way.

Anyway, he knew that this lady would want it that way. And he went on, 'I would like you to keep the children in.'

'That will be easy to do, marshal.'

'Thank you, ma'am.'

'Thank you for warning me.'

He had no rejoinder to that. He tipped his hat and turned on his heels and went on his way.

He heard the schoolhouse door open behind him, heard it close. She had not left it ajar this time. He did not look back. And now he moved into the middle of the main street.

The sun slanted in at him from the left. He would get it more than Whalebone would and that was better for Whalebone than it was for him. But he had to be thankful that it was not right in his eyes. There was nothing he could do about it now anyway. It would have been better if he had moved in from the direction of the jail, as he might have done. But the visit to the school had been an important thing.

Whalebone must have been looking for him. He came down the steps from the hotel and across the boardwalk and walked to the middle of the street and turned to face Amos, and it was quiet and there did not seem to be anybody else about.

20

Whalebone was wanted for murder now: that was a new thing. But the man had gone through with things as he must have planned to do all along. Maybe he figured his string was running out, and this was the to-hell-or-not ploy of a desperate man. And hadn't Whalebone always been a desperate man?

I would have hunted him anyway, Amos thought. Even if it meant going out of my jurisdiction, giving up my badge, I would have hunted him. If needs be, I would have bountied him, it would have come to that. Were Whalebone and he in a sense two of a kind? Desperate men who did desperate things! And was not it inevitable that, one on each side of the fence, they would inevitably clash?

Whalebone was bringing things to a head with a vengeance. And with style. Amos had to admire him for that. In his heart of hearts Amos had known that the man would come. Hadn't he (Amos) said so? The knowledge had, in a small way, eaten at him. He was even sort of grateful to Whalebone for bringing the thing to a head so soon.

The complete shape of the man was not yet particularly clear to him. It was the way the sun was.

Whalebone waited and Amos went slowly closer to him. Whalebone was not exactly a shadow, not what you might call a black cut-out limned against the sun, for the sun was not exactly behind him. But his lean face was indistinct. And Amos liked to watch a man's eyes!

Well, so be it! He picked his stand and he halted. He went through the ritual, as he had done many times before. And Whalebone, wanted killer, could be said to have earned his right to that ritual now.

He (Amos) had not known this man well, but now he addressed him by his first name and in his voice was a sort of mocking courtesy as he said:

'I have to take you in, Jake.'

He did not always wear his star around town but

he had pinned it to his breast this morning and he knew that the sun, the way the sun was, would be shining on it.

Whalebone said, 'If you want me, Amos, I guess you'll have to take me. I'm not coming peaceable.'

Amos did not say anything else. He did not move again for his hands were already lax at his sides, the right one near his holstered Colt Dragoon. He did not even crouch. But Whalebone seemed to lower himself a little. His tall, gaunt form seemed to shorten. Amos waited. He looked as if he were content to wait all morning, only his eyes squinting a little – it might even have been in good humour – as the sun caught them with slanting beams.

'If you want me, come an' take me,' said Whalebone.

'You called the shots,' said Amos. 'You chose the time and the place. Maybe you want to give yourself up.'

Whalebone laughed softly, without humour. Amos went on, unheeding, 'I want you to walk to me and give me your gun.'

'To hell with you,' said Whalebone. But there was no fury in his voice, only a sort of resignation.

He moved then. To Amos it was a sort of blur of motion, the tall figure not so tall, not so big now in the sun. The gunfighter's crouch, the clawlike lift, the bringing level of the heavy gun, a Colt much like Amos's own gun. The blur was not a blur though – that had been a trick of the sun – it was a smoothness. As Amos's own actions were a smoothness. He could not see Whalebone's hooded, shaded eyes. He had reacted only to the man's first, almost infinitesimal movement.

The arm lifting, the gun balanced, the thumbing

of the hammer. The old gunfighter's way. Two men acting as if by some unseen or unheard signal, something that they heard only in their heads, saw there, acted upon like well-oiled machinery. *Two* signals maybe. Their signals to each other.

Amos still upright but twisting slightly now, a lesser target. And his gun out and levelled at the end of a right arm at full stretch but angled downwards a bit, pointing like an accusing finger at the half-crouching Whalebone, pointing at the full of the man's chest as he, for the moment, was a broader target than Amos himself. And two guns bucking and flaming and giving off black, acrid smoke which, as there was no wind, obscured sun and vision so that the two men were then, momentarily, partially hidden from each other.

But Amos knew he had, you might say, beaten Whalebone to the draw, and had hit him, had maybe hit him twice, saw him, as if through swirling blue mist, stagger, half-crumple, becoming a lesser target. But then it was as if an unseen hand caught Amos's gun and jerked it upwards.

He didn't know. Suddenly he didn't know anything! It was as if something had fallen on him, then there was rushing pain in his head. And then there was complete blackness ...

Whalebone hit the ground and it threatened to close over him. But he fought it and he found his feet and he found the sidewalk, blinked at it, lurched forward to it, almost falling on his face, but his momentum carrying him forward, carrying him on, hearing his own heels on the wood drumming like thunder in his head and then fading like his life's-blood. But a sort of blindness driving him on as the blood pumped and he knew it was pumping from him. But he wouldn't die yet – not if he kept moving!

The sidewalk, the turning, the alley where his horse waited. Clambering into the saddle and saying, 'Go, boy'. At least, that was what he meant to say. It was only a whisper. But the horse needed no urging. He went out of that alley like a cannonball. You could depend on ol' Pizenhead for that kind of violent temper, and Whalebone clung to the horse as it carried him away.

Young Lessiter haggled with Jika over the three horses but, after all, had to admit that he didn't get a particularly bad price. He drank tequila with the fat man and he asked about a fat girl: Sukie.

Jika said Sukie had gone and he had learned that Sukie had joined Cornelia Dallahan's stable in Santa Fe. Not that anybody knew what was happening at that stable now, for Cornelia had been shot to death by her old paramour, Whalebone.

Lessiter hadn't known that. Lessiter had once worked briefly with Whalebone, had held the horses for the gang during a raid on an express office in a town. Lessiter couldn't remember the name of the town.

'I was just a tad at the time,' he said.

'You ain't much more than a tad now,' Jika told him.

Lessiter ignored this, asked as a matter of interest where Whalebone was now. Jika said nobody seemed to know where Whalebone was now.

Lessiter said well, to hell with Whalebone

anyway, he'd go to Santa Fe and try and find Sukie, which shouldn't be hard if she was still there as she wasn't the sort you could miss in a crowd, plenty of her an' then some.

'You can bring her back here if you want to,' Jika said magnanimously.

'I might do that,' said Lessiter.

Meanwhile, the earlier subject of his and Jika's cogitations – one Whalebone – was letting his horse carry him where the beast might. Riding in a dream, a nightmare, a world of intermittent agony and spasms of a shadowy near-death, and now and then a light-headed period when he was almost rational. Even then he was not quite sure where exactly he had been hit. It was as if his whole body was on fire. He wanted to scream. But his mouth, it seemed, was too parched. He could only manage an occasional croak. He could not take his hands off the reins, the saddle, could not even manage to reach his canteen. He knew that if he fell from the saddle he was a goner for sure.

He knew he had been hit more than once. He would have expected it. But maybe not this bad. It was bad; oh, mercy, it was very bad! It was even worse than that last time ...

He figured he had got Amos though.

He tried to laugh, and blood spilled from his mouth.

The horse took him and seemed to know where.

It was to the Doombend settlement that old Pizenhead took him and big Ma came out to meet them and she had her big knife in her fist, the blade she used for so many different kinds of things.

21

'He was hit twice,' Rad Spink said. 'Maybe even three times. And they weren't no flea-bites. Anybody who saw it, those I've talked to, they all say that. In the windows. Upstairs an' down. And the undertaker's boy was in an alley. I guess he's peeved – no business for him. Not yet anyway. But I don't think that Whalebone will get far. The way he went across that sidewalk an' got on that horse. The horse took him, some horse that one he'd got!'

'I've see'd things like that during the war,' said stocky Rube. 'I've seen men go for miles with lead in 'em. Enough lead to sink 'em, and usually it did in the end. But not always.'

'He's away anyway,' said Rollo Green. 'Nobody's follering him. He can fall off that horse out there an' the buzzards can have him.'

'I told you ...!' began Rube.

But Deputy Rad cut in, saying, 'Here's Amos now.'

He had a white bandage around his head, his stetson perched somewhat grotesquely upon it. He walked straight and he had a thin, lopsided grin on his lean face bisected by the black moustache.

'A nasty crease,' he said. 'In further and I would've had brain damage an' that wouldn't have done me any good at all.'

'You got a headache, Amos?' asked Rube.

'Some. But riding will help get rid o' that.'

'Where's that goddam Injun now?' said Rube.

As if on cue Lazy came into sight, shambling like a small bear in ragged clobber.

'He saw your smoke signals,' said Rollo.

'Ha, ha!' retorted Rube mockingly. He had found Lazy and asked him to track for them, try and find the horses that had been stolen from the ranch where Rollo worked, find the folks who had killed the ranny who had been Rollo's friend. A bunch of horses like that shouldn't be hard to follow, but a good tracker was mighty valuable and, after Rube finding him, Lazy had, surprisingly, seemed almost eager to hit the trail. He didn't look drowsy now either, though not exactly bright-eyed and bushy-tailed, more like a small old bear who smelled honey.

'Let's go then,' said Amos.

The ranch was but a short ride away and they did it in a short time and Amos didn't wince too much. It was comparatively easy to pick up the trail of the stolen horses and the thieves. Two cowpunchers had already done this but had been told by their boss not to go too far, not to stick their necks out. One of their friends already lay dead on a trestle in the bunkhouse ready for the ministrations of the Golden Bluffs undertaker who would soon be arriving with his boy.

On behalf of the posse, Amos apologized for their tardiness. It had been entirely his fault, he said – and he wouldn't be contradicted by the others. There was something he had had to do. He wouldn't have been able to get out of town otherwise. Come to think of it, he could have been laid low there.

Legend of Amos

When they left the ranch and hit the trail, with Amos in the lead and Lazy by his side, they had three of the cowhands with them, boys that Rollo Green affirmed could prove pretty handy in a pinch.

Lazy seemed a bit in awe of Marshal Amos and more inclined to exchange confidences with Rube whom he now obviously looked upon as his friend.

Lazy gave Rube a sort of side glance and the stocky rider kneed his mount forward and caught up with the old Indian and they exchanged a few words. Then Rube said to Amos, 'He thinks the bunch is being driven towards the Doombend settlement.'

'He figured it might be the Doombend clan who was responsible all along, huh?' said Amos.

'Yeh, could be. Or the thieves could be expecting to drop the stock there for *dinero*.'

In an aside Lazy said something more to Rube, and the latter exclaimed, 'He wants us to stop a bit.'

'All right.' Amos raised a hand for a halt and the party reined in. Lazy went ahead. He had a little spotted cayuse Rube had hired for him from the stables in town. The horse trotted daintily, carefully, as his rider leaned from the saddle and searched the ground, pausing at a small shrubbery, then ranging onwards in a sort of half-circle.

He came back and his eyes were brighter and he approached Rube and barked at him softly, and then Rube said, 'He's found some blood. On the bushes, on the grass. Fresher than last night he thinks. And we ain't heard of any of the horse-thieves getting hurt anyway. Whalebone? He could've gone round the ranch without being spotted. Away from it in fact. And he could've come onto the trail here, maybe even to try an' fool us, if he still had that much sand in him.'

'Maybe the Doombends are old friends of his.'

'That's likely.'

'If it was him o' course. We'll follow on anyway. Let the blood speak for itself later if it can.'

'Sometimes you come out with the damndest things, Amos,' said Rube.

'Your friend ready to move again?'

Lazy heard that and nodded his head and Rube said, 'He's ready.' And Amos gave the signal.

Next time they halted they were in sight of the trees and the draw where the Doombend settlement had its being.

'Spread out,' said Amos.

Then in a long line they went ahead, keeping their horses to a slow trot. There was no cover. They kept low in the saddle and, rifles now loose from saddle-boots, carried them in front of them, and each man with a belt-gun, or more than one, and a knife too maybe.

Lazy had an old Henry rifle across his borrowed saddle and a long knife in a tattered leather scabbard at his belt. A real sharp-pointed pigsticker by the shape of it. Everybody was loaded for bear – and Lazy wasn't the bear.

Suddenly one of the ranch-boys exclaimed, 'Hell, I'll swear that's some of our stock over there,' and he pointed and they all saw the horses in the edge of the trees.

It was Caleb Doombend who first spotted the line of approaching horsemen, and he ran back into the encampment squawling like an old maiden auntie with her pantaloons on fire.

Folks came out of the big hut and Ma was among them and she still had her big knife in her hand, the broad, very sharp blade slimy with red blood.

'Get your guns, all o' you,' she yelled, her voice hoarse as a man's. The polyglot and somewhat ragged company, both male and female, scattered in all directions. Some of them were already well-britched as regards armaments and they ran to the front, Caleb among them, brandishing his rifle which he had grabbed off the rickety porch.

At the moment he was rather in disfavour with Ma who, despite the vengeance that the clan had wreaked on that ranch, couldn't seem to forget the death of Ben and Caleb's hand in it.

He'd show her he was worth his salt, he surely would!

At the first sight of the horsemen he had felt like running, diving for the bushes, lying on his belly, hiding. But Ma had called the tune — and he was going to show them, he was going to show them all!

He was the first to fire a shot, aiming at one of the leading riders, missing him entirely. The bastard swerved, he thought; hell, I would've hit him if he hadn't swerved.

Caleb raised his Winchester to his shoulder again.

Amos was glad that, so far anyway, there were no sharpshooters on the other side comparable to himself or young Rad, and maybe Green.

He knew that the first shot, which had come closer to him than to anybody else but had been little menace to anybody, had been fired by a younker on the edge of the trees. Then, as at his signal his own men opened up, he saw that the younker was hit, his arms reaching for the sky, fingers clawing, his rifle describing an arc, the sun catching it before it fell, and then its owner falling upon it, half-disappearing, a still heap in the grass.

This fatal shot had been fired by Lazy with his old Henry. This old Indian was turning out to be a surprising asset, a surprising character.

And the bunch, following the sweep of Amos's arm, were sitting their horses at a gallop now, but not bunching, still spread out, fanning as they hit the edge of the trees, closing in a bit then though, like curved claws moving to meet.

The outer ring of trees was a higgledy-piggledy, straggly mess littered with refuse and stinking like a midden. And the defenders were moving back to closer cover. It was obvious that they had been taken by surprise. They had not even had a look-out. It was evident they had been carousing. Green had said that the Doombend clan were noted for their tremendous boozing, with old Nat Doombend the champion toper of all and never sober.

There had been a few quite soon out front, including the young man with the Winchester. Passing him, Amos glanced down.

Caleb Doombend – for it was he – had been hit in the throat, must have been dead even before he hit the ground.

The horsemen had the advantage. The defenders, male and female, were all on foot. A rider, probably only a sort of visitor, tried to escape the camp and was shot out of the saddle by one of the ranch-boys. Foot caught in a stirrup, the rider, wounded in the side, was dragged along screaming until he became entangled in underbrush, caught, his mount galloping wildly out onto the plain.

Rube came to grief, if only temporarily. He saw Ma Doombend coming at him, brandishing her knife, which appeared to be bloodstained, glinting oilily in the sun. A grimacing avenging fury, she screamed at him and slashed at his leg but got the horse instead. The beast screamed, an echo of the woman's battle-cry, and reared, throwing its rider. A hoof caught the big woman a glancing blow in the side and she rolled like a large ball.

Rube, scrambling to his feet, lost sight of her, as he was immediately set upon by a tall, gangling character in shirt and pants with a shotgun. The shotgun boomed. A fraction to the right and the charge would likely to have blown half Rube's head off. But the attacker had been too precipitate, or was just a lousy shot. Rube drew his pistol and shot the man in the head.

Momentarily alone, a man dead at his feet and Ma vanished as if the ground had swallowed her, Rube looked around for his wounded horse, couldn't spot him anywhere either.

His rifle was in its scabbard beside his saddle. He had slid it in there when he entered the thicker growth of trees and figured a hand-gun was better. Now he could see ramshackle buildings ahead of him, tents, *hovels*.

The attackers were letting their horses go now and hand-to-hand fighting was in progress, or gun-to-gun, knife-to-knife. Some of the defenders were still in a state of half-dress. The women in particular were demoralized, running, hiding.

They had no leader now. Until Ma, regaining consciousness after surviving a kick in the side from Rube's wounded horse, rose from the underbrush like an avenging spirit. Her bloodstained knife was still in her hand and she glared around her, seeking victims, sacrifices.

Rad Spink was afoot when Ma came at him with the knife.

He raised his gun. At first he thought that the big, ragged, stocky figure was a man. Then he saw it was a woman, Ma no less – though he had never seen her before. And he hesitated. Lawman or not, shooting women was not in his scheme of things.

But the scheme of things now was completely haywire, and Ma had never fitted into any conventional scheme of things anyway. She lunged at Rad with her broad, wicked-looking blade and he side-stepped and she missed him. He swung at her with his gun and he missed too.

But Ma was quicker than she looked and she whirled on him, slashing once more. The blade ripped his shirt and he felt the burn of the steel on his arm, his right arm.

His gun was propelled from his hand. He tried to grapple with the woman. She was bulky, strong, fast. She stank. Her breath was in his face. The weight of her bore on him. He could feel the warm, sticky blood running down his right arm which he couldn't seem to be able to lift anymore.

His face was pressed into Ma's shoulder and she seemed to be hugging him. He now had his left hand around her wrist, striving to prevent her from plunging the blade of the knife into his belly.

Over the woman's shoulder he saw Lazy, afoot, and the old Indian also had a knife in his hand which he now threw in a sort of underhanded motion. Rad had never seen anybody throw a knife in that way before. It wasn't even a throwing-knife: it was Lazy's long-bladed, sharp-pointed weapon

Legend of Amos

that looked like a stiletto.

The big woman stiffened. Her mouth gaped wide, revealing broken yellow teeth. She made a sort of gurgling sound and her eyes rolled, showing the whites. She became boneless, falling away from Rad and he letting her go, recoiling. She hit the ground and he knew she was dead. Not glancing at her again, he retrieved his Colt from the grass.

He looked around for Lazy again, saw the Indian's back as he disappeared into a long, ramshackle building with a sagging porch. Rad followed.

There was an old man sitting on the splintered boards of the porch with his back against the wall. His eyes seemed to be turned up the way Ma's had gone before she died. Rad didn't know whether the old man was dead or not. He didn't appear to have a weapon on him or near him. His mouth was open and spittle drooled down his chin.

Then Rad saw the bottle on its side, the liquor spilling from it. These folks had been having themselves a time, celebrating their thieving no doubt. And this oldster looked as if he had had the biggest time of all. Rad even smelled the hooch now, a sour rotgut smell which was pungent even over the smell of cordite and gunsmoke.

22

Gun in hand, Amos skirted the old shack and came face to face with a big feller who also had a gun and had heard him coming and had the weapon out at arm's length. Because it had seemed comparatively quiet out here – Amos was looking for stragglers – Amos had his Dragoon almost at his side. And even as Amos lifted his Dragoon the other man fired.

Amos lurched to one side and felt the wind of the slug go past his face. He stumbled but, even so, he managed to bring his gun level. He fired twice. The first bullet did not seem to hit. But the second one did.

Plugged in the chest, the other man went backwards as if he had been kicked. His heels did indeed kick up and then he fell flat, the back of his head hitting the ground hard. Amos imagined he could feel the impact in his own aching head. Somewhere he had lost his hat from atop the cocoon of bandages, and even the bandages appeared to have slipped sideways and threatened to block his vision on one side.

A man running through the trees, running away, turned and snapped a shot at Amos. It missed him and chewed wood out of the wall behind him. Amos levelled his gun, thumbed the hammer. The running man did a little skip and Amos saw him drop his gun. But then he disappeared through the trees. Amos wondered how badly he was hit, how far he would get. He didn't follow him. There were movements behind him and he whirled.

A man staggered around the corner, empty-handed, his face running with blood. He tried to say something, didn't make it, collapsed at Amos's feet. Amos had already recognized one of the three rannies who had joined the posse at the ranch. He bent, checked the man's pulse. He was still alive but had been hit in the head and was in a bad way.

Another man came around the opposite corner, spotted Amos, withdrew again like a jack-rabbit into a hole.

Amos took off his vest, rolled it, pillowed the wounded man's head on it. Then he ran after the man who had bolted. There was not much shooting now but there seemed to be a lot of shouting and catterwauling.

Rollo Green ran towards the big shack around which most of the action seemed to be centred, though it seemed there was lull right now. Green had seen Rad Spink go into the big shack and Rad was Green's boyhood friend and Rad might be in danger.

A man came out of the trees at the side of Green as Green ran across the littered clearing. Green, seeing the newcomer out of the corner of his eye, turned but was a little too late. The newcomer had a gun in his hand and he raised it, levelled it, a sure sign that he wasn't one of Green's party but belonged to the other side.

Green raised his gun, but the other man had

already let off a shot and Green's gun remained unfired as the bullet took him in the fleshy part of the shoulder and bored right through. It was Green's left shoulder and he was right-handed but still the power and shock of the wound caused him to drop his gun as he was spun half round, trying desperately to keep his balance.

This was when Amos came around the corner of the shack to discover that his particular quarry seemed to have vanished. But he was greeted by the tableau before him: Green unarmed and still staggering, and his assailant levelling his pistol for another shot.

Hardly pausing to aim himself, Amos let off two rapid shots. He had halted though. He had braced himself, all in that split second. And the two bullets went straight and true and both lodged themselves in their target. The man was thrown backwards in the trees and then only his feet were seen and they were very still.

Amos ran to Green, who was struggling to his feet. He rested on one knee first and looked up at Amos. His eyes were clouded with pain but he grinned with a flash of white even teeth.

'*Gracias, amigo*,' he said.

He held his shoulder and blood squeezed through his laced fingers. 'How bad?' Amos asked.

'No bone touched I don't think,' said Green. 'Went right through.' With his free hand he whipped the kerchief from around his neck and pressed it to the wound.

'I'm with you, marshal,' he said and lurched to his feet.

He followed Amos onto the porch of the big shack. The old man was still there, seated with his

Legend of Amos 155

back against the wall. His eyes were closed now and he seemed to be mumbling to himself.

Green had another comment to make. 'That's ol' Nat Doombend. He ain't gonna hurt nobody. Pore drunken old bastard.'

Behind them somebody called out. Amos turned. Green leaned himself against a sagging post. Two rannies were coming across the littered sod. One said, 'We found the ol' bitch, that Ma. She ain't about to bother anybody any more.'

Somebody coming through the door had another revelation for Amos. It was Rad and he looked a bit pale around the gills. 'Whalebone's in there,' he said. 'What's left of him.'

Rube came into view from the gloom, said, 'Naked and carved. I guess he was still alive when he got here, an' then the woman worked on him. That big old bitch an' her big knife. It ain't pleasant. We covered him with a blanket, Amos.'

'Right.'

'We rounded 'em up in there. I guess some of 'em must've got away, huh?'

'Some,' said Amos. He turned on the two rannies. 'Your pard's round back. He's hurt bad. Do what you can for him.'

They turned and ran. Green let himself slide against the post, down the post to a seated position. He looked owlishly at old Nat Doombend. 'Greetings, pardner,' he said. The old man didn't say anything.

Rad Spink joined Rollo Green. Amos went into the shack with Rube. There were men in there; and some women. A sorry crew, all of them looking pretty unhappy. They were all lined against the far wall and Lazy was facing them, only looked quickly over his shoulder as the other two men came in. He had his Henry rifle at the ready. His long pigsticker was back in his belt.

A blanketed body lay on the trestle table in the middle of the floor. Two feet hung out, a strangely white and almost skeletal pair. One of the men against the wall was moaning, blood dripping from his fingertips.

Amos said, 'Find rope. There should be plenty around. Link 'em together. The women as well. We'll go into the rights an' wrongs of everybody later. Try an' find some bandages, clean rag, anything like that. Look after our people first.'

'I'll get things organized,' said Rube.

'Help him, Lazy. I'll watch this lot.'

'Sure, marshal.'

'And watch yourselves.'

Then he was alone.

'Turn around and face the wall, all of you,' he said.

This was a voice, cold as ice, pitiless: it brooked no argument. They did as the voice told them to do.

'Put your hands behind you and hold them together.'

They did that too.

The weapons had been thrown under the table where the shrouded corpse lay. There was silence now, until the man with the wounded arm began to moan again, a mournful sound. The interior of the shack, though it did not smell at all sweet, was cool and shaded except where the sun slanted in.

Gunsmoke smells cleaner, Amos thought. But even the smell of gunsmoke was wafting away now.

Postscripts

Cornelia Dallahan's place and the area in Santa Fe where that illustrious madam had been Number One was in a state of flux. Notorious clients had tried to take over the cathouse, and the girls. But local constables defending a sideways meal-ticket and helped by various 'friends' who made most of the clients look like tenderfeet, had driven those ambitious characters away. Some of the girls had already taken it upon themselves to find more lucrative venues. They had attended the funeral of their late employer, at which, and its aftermath, a roaring time had been had by all, and then they had gone their separate ways. By gar, Cornelia's place wasn't the only cathouse or like establishment in town anyway! Some of them took the plunge and went free-lance. Fat Sukie, a newcomer anyway, was one of these. She had been a free-lance back in Oatsville – and one of chief Jika's favourites too – so why not in Santa Fe also?

Young Lessiter had more difficulty in finding Fat Sukie than he had expected, but he finally tracked her down to a room in a back-street establishment which grandly called itself an hotel. Sukie wasn't the only girl of her kind there and Lessiter wasn't the only client.

It was late, and Sukie already had a client, a big, cross-eyed, half-mad ex-miner known as Side-away John. Sukie, sloppy frail as she was, had neglected to lock her door. Lessiter, peevish young cuss that he was, and getting more peevish by the minute, marched right in.

Side-away John took umbrage. Buck-naked, he rose from the bed, lifted Lessiter like a doll, carried him onto the landing and threw him down the stairs.

When they picked Lessiter up it was to discover that his neck was broken and that his young life had fled from him. Fat Sukie wailed at the top of the stairs and, half-dressed and carrying the rest of his clobber, Side-away John slunk out the back way and disappeared from the ken of all ...

Weeks later a horse that was said to have belonged to the giant ex-miner was found wandering in the hills. Then a large body was discovered in a jumble of rocks. The corpse could have had a neck quite as broken as young Lessiter's had been, could have been cross-eyed as John had been but, because the vultures had been at it, there was no telling ...

The aftermath of the battle of the Doombend settlement was busy and at first a bit complicated; but things got sorted out. The young ranny who had been badly shot regained his health but walked a mite lopsided for the rest of his life. All other wounds partaken by the law side were subsequently healed. The Doombends had definitely had the worst of it.

Ma was buried where she had lived. Her husband Nat, crying like a drunken baby, wanted to stay with her and was allowed to do so. Then there was no Doombend settlement anymore, except for Nat and a simple girl, a Doombend 'daughter' who looked after him, who found him dead one morning and laid him across a spare horse and toted him into Golden Bluffs. She was allowed to stay there and subsequently worked as a seamstress. But the old man was taken back and buried in a grave next to his wife.

Rube came across Whalebone's silver-grey stallion, Pizenhead, complete with Mex saddle, and with the tacit agreement of Amos took the handsome prize for his own. Man and horse eventually became friends but not before Rube had been bitten in various parts of his anatomy. Subsequently, Rube, the inveterate fiddlefoot (his surname turned out to be Hackersole, which was something he'd never bragged about) decided not to continue to be Amos's would-be third deputy but to, as he put it, go seek his fortune. He didn't stipulate how he might begin to do this. He was in Santa Fe for a while but he didn't stay there. And the rest of the bunch at Golden Bluffs who had shared so much with him ultimately lost touch with him altogether.

Rollo Green finally quit cowpunching and joined his boyhood friend Rad Spink as a second deputy for Marshal Amos. Just after this Rollo married his girl Sadie and Rad married his childhood sweetheart Lila.

It was a double wedding, which Rube Hackersole was able to attend with his now almost-legendary steed, Pizenhead, before they both left. The guests of honour, however, were Amos, Stella, and Stella's daughter Molly. The little girl and her mom looked like a picture in a story-book – as so did the two brides of course. And the grooms were no gargoyles. Amos was very proud of all of them.

Also present among a very large roster of townspeople were storekeepers Harriet and Benjy Kalen, Latten the Street Place barman and his homely half-Indian woman, and for good measure a full-blood Indian known as Lazy.

By now Lazy was working at the Street Place as a sort of swamper-cum-factotum, the other ancient swamper having decided to retire at last. Lazy was almost a pillar of the community now and didn't sleep half as much as he used to.

Word came that the *mestizo jefe* of Oatsville, fat old Jika, had died in his sleep while taking a siesta one hot afternoon ...

Everybody said the West was changing, that the old days were almost gone. The roaring days of the old characters, folks like Rube (and Pizenhead), folks like Whalebone, Jika, Cornelia Dallahan, the Doombends – and even like a legendary law-character, a fighting gunman called Amos ...